I0747371

Arturius
Twisted Tales of Familiar Faces
A.K. Hughey

M4L Publishing

Copyright © 2025 by A.K. Hughey

All rights reserved.

No part of this publication may be reproduced, distributed, or transmitted in any form or by any means, including photocopying, recording, or other electronic or mechanical methods, without the prior written permission of the publisher, except as permitted by U.S. copyright law. For permission requests, contact M4L Publishing, LLC at info@m4lpublishing.com

The story, all names, characters, and incidents portrayed in this production are fictitious. No identification with actual persons (living or deceased), places, buildings, and products is intended or should be inferred.

Book Cover by Natasha Gonzalez

Editing by Melissa Prideaux

First edition 2025

To those brave souls, their names long lost to the shadows of history, who stood their ground, forged hard-won alliances, and gave their lives to save their people.

Note to the reader: A glossary of terms is available at the back of the book for your reference.

Flesh and Bone

IT WAS NOT THE sound of screaming alone nor the rumbling of the earth underfoot that woke Arthur that gray morning. Nay, it was the bone-shaking tones of the war horns resounding through the forest that forced him up out of his bedroll and sent him leaping for his spatha. There wasn't even enough time to don his antique chain mail, an inheritance passed down over five generations.

"Rise!" he shouted to his warriors, voice booming through the forest clearing where they slept amidst a circle of ancient stones known as the King's Men. "On your feet! Spears and shields ready!"

His two wives were among the first to launch themselves out of their bedding and grab their weapons. Rigana, his first wife, renowned for her prowess with the gwayw spear, readied her shield and weapon before kicking at anyone near her who hadn't yet risen. "Arise, bastards, and have a chance at dying on your feet!"

Talara, his second wife, was ready with her short bow within seconds, her eyes wide and face set.

A crashing through the brush in the forest beyond the clearing caught everyone's attention. Some froze in anticipation. Others—like his wives—grabbed their weapons. Arthur slid his spatha from its sheath and took a fighting stance, while his warriors readied themselves. He was poised to swing, slice, and stab at whoever dared appear at the mouth of the trail.

But the face that appeared was feminine, ash-smudged, and tear-streaked. A woman clutching a young child to her chest ran into the clearing and stumbled to a stop when she spotted the ready warriors with their weapons pointed at her. Her tired eyes were wide with shock and fear, and her mouth moved as if she meant to speak but could not.

"Talara," Arthur called softly, but she was already moving to greet the woman.

"M-my daughter. Please—" she gulped hard, "please help her. The Saxons..." She couldn't finish her sentence, her pain too great.

"They're coming this way?" Arthur asked.

The woman only nodded, a fresh burst of tears falling.

Talara shouldered her bow and cradled the child's limp body in her arms. "Come. We have a healer. There is still hope."

With that, Talara turned and headed for the western end of the clearing, the woman following close behind with a fast, limping walk.

A few more refugees entered the clearing from the forest trail as Arthur stood close by and watched with vigilance, urging his people to don their armor and prepare for battle. But before enough were armed and armored to form a shield wall at the mouth of the path, the first of the Saxons charged through, diagonal streaks of blue chalk paint slathered across his face, war axe raised high, and eyes wild with bloodlust. His sudden halt as he ran into the clearing, and the change in his expression when he spotted the number of gwaywffyn pointed in his direction, made it clear to Arthur that the Saxons hadn't been expecting resistance from a band of native warriors.

Before the man could fully register the situation, Arthur closed the distance and thrust his sword through the man's throat. Blood sprayed from the wound, coating Arthur's sword arm, and warm flecks landed on his cheek. Any scream the man might have let out to warn his fellows was reduced to a choking gurgle as the man dropped to his knees. He stared up at Arthur with fierce, crystal-blue eyes, his pupils so large he almost looked inhuman. Placing one foot on the man's chest for leverage, Arthur took the hilt of his spatha in both hands and pulled it free.

The man dropped his axe to the earth with a thud and clasped his hands to his throat, the blood spurting between his fingers to the rhythm of his weakening pulse. Someone shouted, but Arthur shot up a hand to halt them. He turned and shook his head, sliding his gaze across the group of his closest companions, mostly men, but with a handful of the hardest women he'd ever known, aside from his own mother. To his surprise and slight disappointment, it was Lanslot who'd been ready to cheer for Arthur's slaying of the Saxon.

Arthur motioned the ready warriors forward, Rigana at the fore-front of the mass with her thick red hair braided behind her. Talara remained at the far edge of the clearing, beyond the circle of King's Men, as she cared for the refugees and aided the healer. The little girl she'd carried for the first refugee woman now sat against a tree with her eyes open as she sipped from a waterskin.

The sight of her bolstered Arthur's resolve. Such a frail thing, but she'd come back from the brink. She shouldn't have had to, but these bastards from over the sea had a thirst and greed to take all that the Ro-mans had left behind, just as the Scots and Picts had tried to do. Those latter tribes had been trouble to fend off, but the Saxons, Angles, and Jutes were ever fiercer fighters and far more numerous. Their southern cousins had long before sacked Rome and sent the shattered remnants of the Empire running east to Constantinople over one hundred and fifty years earlier. Such fighting forces had well proved the folly of underestimating one's enemies.

Just as Arthur's fighters moved forward, a rumble reverberated in the ground, and the snapping of twigs and branches echoed through the forest. With a sharp movement of his wrist, Arthur flicked much of the blood from his sword, then readied it in both hands before calling to his warriors, "Spears ready!"

When the Saxon at the front of the wave ran into the clearing, Arthur swung his sword at the man's throat with all his might. The blade struck its target, slicing clean through the man's throat and only meeting resistance at the spine. It wasn't enough to stop the blade, though, not with the momentum of the Saxon running in and the force of Arthur's swing. The man's head flew free of his body, spinning up in the air as the body continued forward without it. The headless corpse continued a few feet until the legs gave out, and it plowed chest-first into the dirt, limbs twitching and fingers in a death grip around the handle of the sword the man carried.

As the rest of the wave filed in through the narrow choke point where the path exited the forest, Arthur's spearmen rushed forward over the beheaded Saxon with their shields ready, giving Arthur time and space to get back into the fight. The clangs of metal against metal and the thuds of bodies smashing into shields rang in Arthur's ears, and the metallic scent of blood flooded the air. Grunts and screams resounded as Arthur's warriors clashed with the Saxons, and the sound spurred him into the fray.

He was taller than any other man on his side or the enemy's, with a breadth of well-trained body to match, and the shock of his stature often gave him the advantage when anyone dared face him. He had that effect now, as a black-haired Saxon ducked and dodged spear thrusts until he made enough space from the main fight to square himself to Arthur. His menacing grin half faltered as he looked up to meet his opponent's gaze.

Arthur set his feet, gripped his sword tightly, and, for a moment, wished he'd prioritized donning his armor. The man with the raven hair bolted forward and thrust his sword at Arthur's chest, but was blocked and directed away by Arthur's blade. He gritted his teeth, arm aching as the hilt buzzed with the force of the impact, and he shoved forward with his shoulder, knocking the Saxon back a stride. Adrenaline rushed through Arthur's veins in the cool morning air, invigorating his senses, and he took advantage of the rush.

He swung, blocked, parried, and thrust, blow after blow coming faster until the Saxon panted with exhaustion, his sword arm trembling with the weight of his weapon. Arthur moved into the man's space beneath his swinging sword arm and thrust the spatha blade under the overlapping leather armor and upward into the man's chest before twisting it. Someone slammed into Arthur's shoulder and knocked him backward, but he held tight to the hilt of his spatha, taking it with him and half-pulling the dying Saxon with him until the blade wrenched free of the man's flesh.

Arthur fell on his back with a thud as he hit the earth, gaze searching for his attacker. He found the blade of an axe swinging toward his face, so he rolled away and scrambled to his feet, keeping his tingling fingers wrapped around his sword hilt. Standing, he found that he was closer to the forest than the King's Men where his people were, the enemy now standing between them.

This man was larger than the rest, nearly eye to eye with Arthur, and matching his mass in body. He was almost entirely naked except for a cloth wrapped around his groin, his body painted in blue with white spirals from head to toe. His taut muscles tensed and twitched as he spread his arms wide and roared his violent battle cry. The man's sandy blond hair was long and braided, his dilated pupils surrounded by hazel irises wild with the fury of the battle continuing around them.

With an axe in each hand, the man bared his teeth, jumped forward, slashing both axes at Arthur's middle, but Arthur leapt backward, dancing away from the razor-sharp blades. He could feel the whoosh of air disturb his clothes as the weapons passed too close for comfort. With a flick of his wrist, Arthur thrust his blade at the man's throat, but the blade was pinged away by one of the axes.

This blue bastard was fast and strong, but Arthur didn't allow it to strike fear in him. He'd faced worse over these past ten years. He blocked blow after blow as the heavy axes came swinging for his head, but he was forced backward with each successful defense from the fast, strong attacks. His sword hand was tingling from the shock of the blows. Though the metal was strong—old Roman steel that wouldn't be ruined by the less refined weaponry of the Saxons, Angles, and Jutes—Arthur was as much flesh and bone as any other man, and combat could only be sustained so long before pain and exhaustion drained a man's reserves.

Arthur noticed a weakness in the man's attack pattern; he'd swing left, right, left, right, then haul back his arms and swing with both. It was a near-perfect pattern with just enough breathing room for Arthur to exploit. So he blocked, waited, counted the steps.

Left, right. Left, right. Breathe, and ready those axes for me.

Arthur rushed forward, blade leading, and thrust through the blue man's stomach until the blade exploded from his back. The man's face melted from fury to shock and denial. One axe lowered, the second dropped from his hand, and he half-stumbled in place, glaring down at the blade of the spatha piercing his body. He dropped his other axe, then grabbed at the blade of the spatha with his hands, coughing up blood as he tried to pull the weapon out.

Yanking the sword out of the man, Arthur stepped to the side and watched him fall to his knees, his fingers clutching at his intestines as they spilled from the gut wound. He tried to grab his innards, slippery with blood and gore, but failed to keep them off the ground.

It was a hard way to go. Arthur had watched too many men suffer gut wounds. It was a slow way to die, and he'd never seen anyone survive such injuries, so he turned away, shoving the knowledge of the misery and inevitability to the back of his mind. But as he turned his attention toward the remnants of the battle, he found a Saxon spear en route to his unarmored chest. He barely flicked his sword up in time to knock the tip away, and it grazed his right side, opening a wound along his ribs. Arthur gasped as the pain lit like fire in his flesh, and he stumbled to the left.

Gathering his mind and pushing away the pain, Arthur rushed the spearman before the man could pull back and build up momentum for another stab at him. The distance was too short for Arthur to fully raise his sword for a proper swing with enough strength behind it to finish the job, so he rammed into the man, tucking his head down at the last minute. The impact of the crown of Arthur's head against the unprotected face broke the man's nose, and Arthur slammed the man into the ground, going down with him. Straddling his dazed opponent, Arthur lifted his sword with both hands, blade pointing down.

Before he could pull the sword down with all his might and end the spearman, something hit Arthur's sword, knocking it out of his hands, and before he could react, he was hit in the side of his head. Pain flared through his skull, and white light blinded him. He was vaguely aware of tumbling away and hitting the ground, but he couldn't see, couldn't feel the earth beneath him, couldn't hear anything but a high-pitched ringing.

Arthur tried to groan, tried to roll, willed his legs to work, his arms to move, and his fingers to grasp for something—anything—with which to defend himself. But he was sluggish, his limbs like anchors sinking him beneath the waves of a dense fog that stifled his senses. Everything felt so far away. All his worries, his troubles, and his quest for vengeance for his ravaged family and their people.

He saw her then, the Raven Goddess. The Morrigan.

One raven perched on a shoulder, the other on an outstretched arm. Her long red hair was wild and wind-blown, and her body armored in dark leather and chain mail. Her green-eyed gaze bore into him as the twisted, curled tendrils of her hair whipped around her face and shoulders. She pointed with her free hand toward the ground, and his armor came into focus. It sat in a dirty, bloody heap near a river.

No, Arthur tried to say, but he was too weak to speak the words. *Not yet. I am not finished yet!*

Free the Sword

THE MORRIGAN LOWERED HER arm, shook her head softly, and, in the next instant, knelt beside him, her piercing gaze still boring into him. She waved a hand over his head and hair, and a sudden, fierce warmth washed through him, starting from his head and spreading through his body, down to the tips of his fingers and all the way to his toes.

"Rise, Arturius, son of Uther, grandson of Ambrosius Aurelianus." The words caressed his mind like a whisper, though her lips never parted. "You must rise. I shall not wash your armor today, mortal."

He studied her face in wonder, questions bursting the seams of his mind. *Why?*

"There are many who would see you become our champion. You must prove you are worthy. Rise to the glory of your ancestors, your name, your future line."

She lowered her face to his, brushed her lips against his cheek, and whispered something in a language he didn't recognize, though it sounded vaguely similar to the secret tongue of the druids. As she finished, she laid a hand on his chest, and an icy jolt of energy coursed through his veins, shocking him with every pulsing beat of his heart.

Arthur bolted upright, sucking heaving breaths into his aching chest, body trembling as he regained consciousness. A war cry drew his vision into sharp focus, and he found a man standing over him with a gleaming sword raised high, bloodlust glittering in his dilated pupils. Instinct screamed at Arthur to roll away or to strike first, but his limbs were heavy as the jolt of adrenaline bled away and the goddess's icy touch ached in his bones.

He grabbed the handle of something that pressed against his leg to block the sword his opponent thrust toward Arthur's skull. It never reached him. The swordsman froze, weapon still raised, when an arrow sank into his face, embedding in the inner corner of the eye socket. His lips contorted with pain, and his fingers twitched, his sword falling loose from his grip. Arthur flung himself to the side as the sword clattered to the ground, less than a finger's width from his head.

Pushing himself off the ground, Arthur stood as many hands came to his aid. Though he still trembled, he tried to wave them off.

"Are you trying to get yourself killed, Arturius?" Rigana asked, her voice raspy and deep. She used his formal name, Arturius, in front of the rest of the warband, but she called him Arthur when they were alone.

"Nay, wife. Do you think I'd leave all the glory to you?"

She snorted and rolled her eyes. "We both know it's not about glory."

"Aye. We do. But no, the first of my loves, I was not tempted to leave you to travel alone in this world."

Rigana said nothing, but her jaw clenched, and she swallowed hard. He wanted to comfort her both with his words and his body, but they maintained a certain decorum in battle and warfare. Both his wives were his faithful soldiers when they were out here with him, and they were as professional and steadfast as the best of his men.

"Talara," he asked, turning until he found her glistening gray eyes staring at him.

"I couldn't risk it," she said, bristling. "After you got hit, I couldn't just let him—"

Arthur raised a hand to silence her, wincing inwardly at the fact that he couldn't comfort her either. "You judged right, and your aim was true."

That was as close as he could come to showing his gratitude, at least in front of his warriors. He'd ensure she knew his gratitude when they were alone.

She blinked back the tears still welling in her eyes, then nodded sharply.

"We have a few injuries, but none fatal," Lanslot reported, still catching his breath. "I don't know how, but we got damn lucky."

Arthur wanted to say he'd seen the Morrigan, that she'd refused to wash his armor, that she'd come to him in the place between worlds, but his breath caught in his throat, and he could only swallow the words. "Where is my sword?"

"It landed near the King Stone." Lanslot gestured toward the largest stone set outside the ring of the King's Men stones. Near to the King Stone stood another cluster of ancient stones. The old ones called these stones the Whispering Warriors. "The druid stopped us from retrieving it for you."

"Anieras!" Arthur stretched his neck and rolled the growing soreness out of his shoulders.

The withered old druid limped forward, leaning heavily on his staff. His traditional dark brown hooded robe was embroidered with green thread in the shapes of vines and trees up his wide sleeves, and his intricately carved staff crowned with a fist-sized clear quartz wrapped in vines and sinew. The man's weathered face was deeply etched with lines that betrayed his long years of hardship and hard-won wisdom.

"Dux Bellorum." His hoarse voice was shaky as he tipped his head.

"My sword?"

"The sword of your forefathers was flung from battle, and it calls you from the foot of the King Stone. Only you are to touch it."

"This is what the gods say?"

The druid nodded, raised one trembling hand, and pointed to the King Stone. "They did not save my forebears, but they now remember the folly of sitting idly by while invaders steal their lands, destroy their altars, and slaughter their people."

Arthur believed in the gods, but he'd always been wary of those who claimed to be druids. The order had been almost entirely wiped out, with only a handful surviving the systematic slaughter of their kind. All efforts to rebuild and re-people their society had been altogether unsuccessful. They were a dying breed, and a crucial piece of their ancient knowledge was lost every time one of them passed to the next world. So those who remained were, at best, rarely in possession of the full knowledge and wisdom for which they'd been revered in the past.

"And what will the gods ask of me? My sword? My blood? More of the blood of my people?" Even as he balked at the idea, he could still feel the ice-cold caress of the Morrigan's lips on his cheek. Yes, he knew the gods were real, and he believed with all his spirit that at least one of them was by his side, at least for now. Of course, the fact that she was the goddess of battle and death did not provide him much in the way of comfort.

"You should ask the gods what they require, Dux Bellorum."

Arthur repressed a tired sigh. The title of warlord had been made famous by one of his ancestors, and the druid insisted upon calling him by it in every single interaction, regardless of Arthur's request to be called Arturius. His given name struck a balance between both the

Kernow and Roman lines of his ancestry, and it reminded others he was a man bred, born, and raised to wage war.

"You truly mean that no one else may retrieve my sword?"

"The sword of your father may be freed from the King Stone by none but you."

Did he feel like testing the druid and the old gods today? After nearly dying twice before the sun had even broken the fog today, he found he did, in fact, feel lucky enough to tempt fate again. He ran his tongue over his teeth, then spat blood on the ground.

"Lanslot, my oldest friend," Arthur said, keeping his gaze locked on the druid's emotionless face.

"Yes, Arturius?"

"Retrieve my spatha."

Lanslot nodded sharply, then jogged to the King Stone and halted before the sword, which was planted point-down in the earth at the base of the stone, just as the druid had said. He reached out his hand, hesitated, then slowly wrapped his fingers around the hilt.

Nothing happened.

The man's chest deflated as he exhaled his relief, and he tightened his grip, then pulled. To everyone's surprise, the sword didn't budge. Lanslot grasped the hilt with both hands, leaned back, braced with one foot, and pulled with all his might. His neck muscles strained, and a vein bulged in his forehead beneath stray wisps of his short, dark brown hair. His grip on the sword faltered, and he fell backward suddenly, landing hard on his ass. "Damn it!"

"Bah! Let me try," Drystan said, playfully kicking Lanslot as he passed. "You're hardly considered the strongest man among us."

Laughing haughtily, he took his place before the King Stone, rubbing his hands on his leggings before wrapping them around the hilt of the sword, bending his knees, and using his whole body to try and wrest the sword out of the earth.

Arthur stifled a chuckle, sore as he was, watching his closest friends and best warriors struggle to prise the sword free. Rigana tried as well, and Talara followed immediately after. Both met the same result as the rest of his people, though neither was bothered as much as his men. It became a bit of game, and even the young bard Myrddin tried his hand. As usual, he made a show of it by falling on his rear and rolling backward before springing up like a hare, making everyone laugh.

"Enough," Anieras grumbled, shaking his staff at the lot of them before pointing the quartz at Arthur. "You mock the gods by making them wait on you with these games."

"My apologies, wise one." Arthur dipped his head in deference, sighed, and strode to the King Stone. The surface of the ancient rock had once been carved, but the wind, rain, and snow had long worn away the lines. He could barely make out the ancient etching of a man's face. It wouldn't be much longer before any sign of the carved visage of the king had eroded entirely.

Mist still clung to the edges of the clearing, and the sea of limitless gray above them filtered what should have been the warm light of a spring sun. The blade of his spatha reflected the cool light, gleaming in the few places where blood hadn't dried on it. A cool breeze stirred, teasing the wet locks of Arthur's hair onto his face. He brushed them away, took one more glance at his people, and steeled himself. He refused to show fear or hesitation in front of them, so he reached smoothly for the hilt, his hand strong and steady.

Arthur's fingers curled around it, and every muscle in his hand spasmed, tightening painfully until he felt his fingers would break. A burning heat shot up his arm, racing through his veins until it struck his head and blurred his vision. He gasped, dropped to his knees, and clutched his free hand over the other on the hilt. The voices of his people rose in hysterics all around him, but they sounded farther away than they should have.

Something grasped him by the back and forced his head forward. Though he fought it, whatever compelled him was undeterred. On his knees, he bowed his head, and with his vision gone to darkness, he only had the strength left to part his lips and whisper Her name. "Morrigan."

A gust of warm wind blew hard against his face, smothering his breath and pulling at his skin. He felt himself moving, his stomach sinking with a sensation he'd only felt as a boy when he'd been thrown from his horse. When he opened his eyes, he was greeted by a landscape of lush grass whipping in the wind.

Arthur looked out over a land he didn't recognize from the vantage point of a hilltop, and turned slowly, taking in the semi-circle of trees and the odd beings standing crowded together in front of them. Dread filled him as his gaze met the cold, gray orbs fixed on him. There were no irises or pupils, only a chalky grayness covering the whole of the eyeball. Their skin was youthful, plump, and healthy, their faces expressionless.

Three of the beings slipped through the crowd until they reached the front. He recognized the Morrigan immediately, her arms at her sides and a raven perched on one shoulder. Her eyes were also strange, missing the irises and pupils he remembered from his earlier vision, but instead of chalky gray, hers were a glistening black, like pieces of jet plucked from a stream. She stood between two males.

On her right stood a giant man with long, wavy dark hair, cloaked in a red cape, holding a spear pointing upward in his left hand. In his right hand, he gripped the reins of a black horse twice the size of the largest Arthur had ever seen. Both the man and the horse had glowing red eyes that bore into him with a heat reminiscent of what he'd felt when he grabbed his sword.

To the left of the Morrigan stood a man in a green cloak, an ancient-looking short bow in one hand and the other hand resting on the head of an enormous wolf sitting faithfully on his left side. Their eyes glowed green, but the sensation washing over Arthur was one of relief and understanding rather than one of fear.

"He is our champion," he heard a woman's strong voice insist, though none of the figures moved their mouths or parted their lips.

"His lineage is sullied by the sons of Romulus." The Hunter and his wolf both sneered at him.

"That strengthens him." The Warrior slammed the butt of his spear into the earth, and a rumbling flowed from it. "There is no one better."

"And what if he should turn to their old gods, or worse, their new one?"

"We have little—"

A crack of thunder shattered the calm of the clearing, so loud Arthur shut his eyes and covered his head. The thunder rumbled in waves as it dissipated, but the warm wind grew colder. When he opened his eyes again, the beings that had stood behind the three arguing had disappeared. In their place squatted a giant man wearing black robes and a helmet topped with white antlers. Its long horns sprouted from the brushed iron, spreading and twisting until they ended in too many sharp points to count.

Whatever eyes the giant had were hidden in the shadows behind his helmet's nose-guard, but his entire form pulsed with a soft white glow. The air around the giant thrummed with energy, and Arthur could feel it in his astral bones.

The giant rose to his feet, hefting an iron club from the earth in his right hand, as a giant stag emerged from the forest on his left. The

Morrigan, the Warrior, and the Hunter all moved aside and knelt, bowing their heads to the horned god. Each step of the giant shook the earth and sent a rumbling wave rolling through the hills as he approached Arthur.

Into the Wild Places

THE SHADOWS THAT SHOULD have contained eyes bore down on Arthur, and he had enough intelligence to imagine himself kneeling to greet the ancient deity. It worked, and his astral self knelt, though he couldn't tear his gaze away from the creature, feeling chained by some strange power. Waves of its humming energy pulsed through his spirit, drawing him in with dual senses of awe and foreboding.

After a few massive strides, the giant halted and bent down, peering at Arthur from the unending darkness of the shadows in its face. It froze for a moment, then nodded its head, the antlers above shaking so hard that bits of stag velvet dusted Arthur's face. The stag snorted and pawed the earth as the giant slowly raised his iron club overhead.

An existential dread flooded through Arthur as he watched the club rise higher. Had the old god approved of Arthur, or hadn't he? The club paused its upward swing, and fell down, blasting into the ground beside Arthur, shaking his entire body and sending him sprawling.

Arthur slammed into the ground, bouncing backward with his eyes squeezed shut, tumbling again and again until he thudded against something solid and unmoved by his momentum. His sore ribs and back throbbed, and he sucked shuddering breaths into his burning lungs. Sounds started coming back to him, muffled at first, then clearer as he regained full consciousness.

"Dux Bellorum!"

"Arturius!"

"Husband? Ah, he's fine."

He opened his eyes to find many faces staring at him from above. Anieras, Lanslot, Drystan, and Rigana.

"Arthur?" a softer voice called, almost too quietly to hear.

Dropping his gaze, Arthur saw Talara kneeling at his left side, her eyes wide with fear, bottom lip quivering.

"I'm here." He took her hand in his own and squeezed it.

The feeling of falling and rolling hadn't left him entirely, but the aching fingers of his free hand brought the realization that he held something. He looked to his right and found he gripped his sword, and the old spatha shone with a white aura that pulsed in time with his heartbeat.

"Do you see it?" Anieras asked, pushing nimbly through the crowd to crouch and examine the spatha.

"I see..." Arthur swallowed the words, worried he'd hit his head too hard to trust his eyes. "What happened to me?"

"You grabbed your sword," Talara explained softly. "Then you looked as if some unseen force had struck you, and you were thrown backward."

"And you freed your sword," Lanslot added with a grin. "The only man who could do it, just as the druid said."

Arthur pushed himself upright, grabbing Drystan's offered arm to rise to his feet. His hand shook as he lifted his sword, but he slowly sheathed the glowing blade anyway. He stumbled forward, pushing the crowd of men and women away as he made his way back to the

King Stone. It swirled now with alternating rings of black, red, green, and white energies. And he saw it then.

The face of a man appeared in the stone, his visage ghostly, as if his spirit peered out from within it. He looked straight at Arthur, his dead-eyed gaze somehow burning into the living man, but motioned Arthur toward him with one shadowy, translucent hand. It had been a hell of a day already, but Arthur knew more than his own pride—his own life—hung on these omens and signs from beyond the world of the living, so he complied. He stood before the stone once more, looking up into the ancient king's misty face.

"Make the Eagle your friend," the ghost king said, though his lips never moved. "Welcome the Siren. Champion the Witch. When you have done all three, you may call upon the power of the dragon, young king, on the dawn of the seventh day."

With that, the ancient spirit faded with a sudden gust of wind, his face no longer visible within the weathered surface of the rock.

"A dragon?" Arthur mumbled, shaken by what he'd seen and heard.

"Arturius?" It was Rigana who took him by the arm first, pulling him away from the King Stone. "Break free of this spell, husband!"

He stumbled backward but kept his balance, then shook his head and rubbed his eyes before turning to his people. Their stricken, pale faces stared back at him, wide-eyed and speechless.

"Anieras," he barked, slapping a hand on Rigana's strong shoulder to steady himself.

The druid hobbled forward as quickly as his aged body allowed. "Yes, Dux—"

"The gods..." He stopped himself, aware of his people with their stares fixed on him. "Walk with me."

"Of course."

To the rest of his people, Arthur shouted, "Make a totem of three heads, an offering to the Morrigan. Lay the other bodies at the King Stone, his Whispering Warriors, and offer whatever remains at intervals around the circle of the King's Men."

He patted Rigana's shoulder and nodded toward the others. There was an unspoken language between lovers, and between them, they knew he meant for her to ensure his orders were carried out properly. She was pious, especially when it came to the Morrigan, and would have the offering properly made without Arthur's oversight, so Arthur pulled the druid along and moved toward a far edge of the clearing, finding a fallen tree on which they could sit.

"The ancient king," Arthur started, swallowing hard as the ghostly face flashed behind his eyes. "I was given instructions. Befriend the Eagle." Arthur shook his head again, dizzy. The encounter was already beginning to feel like a dream, and one that was fading fast. "Welcome the Siren. Champion the Witch. And then I might..."

"Yes?" Anieras encouraged, his pale blue eyes searching Arthur's face."

"He said I may call the Dragon."

Every movement halted in the druid's body, on his face, even the searching twitches of his eyes. He sat as still as if he'd been carved from stone, his stony gaze looking through Arthur rather than at him. A gust of wind rattled the still-bare branches of the trees, and their mighty trunks groaned and creaked.

Arthur felt eyes upon him, the eyes of predators, of things unseen that could rip him apart if he dared take one step too far into the forest by himself. A chill crept down his back as he waited for the druid to speak, and he tried to swallow, but his throat was dry.

"This is my land, damn it." He turned his head to glare into the shadows between the trees and growled. "It's my land! I fight for you! I fight for us!"

Arthur's creeping fear turned to fire as fast as dry grass took the flame, and his fingers clenched so tightly that his nails bit into his palms. He hardly noticed, so incensed was he that they would dare question him.

They? Who are they? He felt as if he was losing his mind.

"They wish to see you prove it, young king."

Anieras's suddenly powerful voice brought Arthur back to the present. The wind no longer blew so harshly, the trees no longer moaned at him, the shadows retreated into the wild places.

"Young king? That's what he said." Arthur tipped his head toward the King Stone. "But I am no king, and I have no wish to be."

"Your parents were both born to families of wealth and power, both lineages drawn to leadership as the bird is drawn to the sky."

Arthur couldn't care less about power and wealth. If the invaders were allowed to continue their reign of terror and the extermination of his people, then there would be no kingdom left to lead. "The Eagle, the Siren, and the Witch. And," he stretched his neck either way, "the Dragon."

"If you accept this quest, you will prove yourself worthy of the land, its spirits, and its peoples. And if you can accomplish this, then all that you now desire can be achieved."

"All that I desire? I want the war, the death, the fires to stop, druid," Arthur grumbled, struggling to keep his voice low. "I want my people to be free, for our way of life to continue into the years."

"Everything ends, Dux Bellorum," the old man said, his voice withering back to normal as he spoke the words. He looked out over the men beheading the fallen Saxons. "I fear that in a hundred years, my kind will already be part of the legends."

"What are you doing about it?"

Anieras shrugged. "More important than the secret rites is the survival of our people. Our people will keep the land, the land will keep the spirits, and the gods will keep and be kept by all. As long as our blood carries on, some part of us, as small as it may be, goes with them."

"Aye." Arthur watched as the three heads were stacked and impaled in front of one of the Whispering Warriors. "If the gods keep all, then why would they give me this task?"

"It is a great circle, Dux Bellorum. When one piece falters, all will crumble, toppling one after another."

"Like allies?"

Anieras nodded, then closed his eyes.

"So, where should we find an eagle?"

"*The* Eagle."

"You have one in mind?"

"I will." Anieras stood, pulled the hood of his robes over his head, and wandered into the forest.

Arthur watched as he went, a shiver rolling through his body when it seemed the wild, gnarled roots of the trees retreated to clear a path for the old man.

Bind the King

WITH THE FINGERS OF his right hand, Arthur smeared cooling Saxon blood over the stones. He started with the King Stone, marking it with ogham lines as the young bard Myrddin had shown him. The apprentice surveyed all the offerings of the dead enemies' bodies and the blood markings on the stones while his master, Anieras, was away in the forest. Of course, the only stone he wouldn't even come close to was the King Stone. Everyone kept as much distance as they could from the ancient rock.

Arthur was aware that the king's spirit within the stone was dormant again, but he didn't bother telling anyone else. He knew in his heart that the old king deserved both respect and rest. So he let the others be afraid while he focused on his work painting the sharp lines. The blood became harder to work with as it cooled and dried, tacky on his fingers and more difficult to make crisp marks.

He dug his fingers into the spear wound between the neck and the shoulder of the Saxon body lying at the base of the King Stone and boldened his ogham. The coppery smell of the blood heightened when touched to the pitted rock face, clinging to Arthur's nostrils and turning his stomach. He'd been in plenty of skirmishes that could have been called a bloodbath, but this was almost too much. And with every symbol finished, he felt the air grow heavier around him. These were not mere symbols, inert and decorative. They were sacred marks that woke the land with its offering. Only his desperation to save his people kept him on his horrific task.

"We better move quickly," he told Myrddin as he completed the ogham. "And next time, we must do this work immediately."

"Maybe next time you won't go messing about, playing with spirits and talking to gods," Myrddin grumbled as he walked away to help with the script on the Whispering Warrior stones. Although he wasn't that much younger, Arthur had always thought of the apprentice as still being a youth. It could have been the boyish grin he wore too often, his wiry frame, the poorly cut golden blond hair that hung in waves to his shoulders, or his immature banter. He didn't act his age, and he'd never looked it either. Arthur might have begrudged him once, but after all the death and suffering they'd seen, he envied the resilience of Myrddin's spirit.

Arthur let him go without scolding his grumbling and focused on the task at hand, or rather, the blood at hand. He made the strikes and motions of the ogham—down, then up, left to right, from bottom to top in diagonal lines—and ensured each swipe was thickly painted. The blood activated the essence of the ogham, as if the symbols drank in this sacrifice of enemy vitality. When he finished, he wiped his hands in the moss and grass, then stepped back to examine his work. Moderate blood drips added almost a softness to the harsh red streaks, but the script was perfectly legible to those who could read it: *Alim*, *Bile*, and *Ruis*.

"This will bind the king and his warriors?" he asked as Myrddin appeared at his side.

"Yes. To the land itself, and the protection of the land," he answered, studying the lines on the King Stone. "It doesn't so much bind them as an unwilling person may be bound in rope and chain. This simply reaffirms their connection to the land, the people, and the spirits."

It pained Arthur to think the king's spirit wouldn't find the rest it had earned. "But—"

"It protects them, too," Myrddin added. "They'll probably be here for at least a thousand years after we've all returned to the earth. He'll get his rest."

"You knew what I would ask?"

Myrddin shrugged. "Maybe the old man has taught me more than I've wanted to admit."

Arthur felt the guilt lifted from his shoulders. He glanced at the face of the stone, where the lines had been worn away and where he'd seen the ghostly visage. There was something about the face and about the feeling of the spirit that had sparked a sympathy in Arthur. He didn't want the old king to suffer anymore.

"And how will they protect this place?"

Myrddin lifted his hands, tilted his face to the heavens, turned in a slow circle, and said in a mocking voice, "This is the way of things. It is the circle of life, death, and all things. Without one, they all fall. Together, they create an unending cycle."

"What would the old man say if he heard your insolence?" Arthur asked, his voice low and conspiratorial.

Myrddin winced briefly, but grinned anyway. "As long as he doesn't hear it, then perhaps we'll all live another day."

"What's left to be done? I'd like to get away from here to make camp."

"Nothing. The other stones are all finished as well. Your wives are quite skilled at writing the ogham."

"I'm glad to hear it. And what of your master? When do you think he'll return with our next instructions?"

Myrddin shrugged, and a smirk lit across his face. "I could play us a song while we wait."

"No!"

"I'm disappointed, great warlord! I must improve as a bard in the same way you improve as a warrior: through practice. The only way I can improve my craft is by playing my lyre."

"I'm sorry, Myrddin, but you're shite at music. You'd best stick to chanting."

"Hey, now! That's harsh."

"I only speak the truth," Arthur said, turning away and walking toward the Whispering Warriors to hide his grin.

"I'll be a legendary bard someday, Arturius! Then who'll be laughing?"

Before Arthur could reach the huddled stones, the sound of someone crashing through the brush caught his ear. It was a faraway sound at first, but quickly grew louder until everyone had drawn their weapons and readied themselves for another fight.

He turned toward his people and brought the raised finger of one bloody hand to his lips. If more enemies were coming their way, he wanted the advantage of surprise. Arthur scrubbed his hands on his trousers, then pulled his spatha from its sheath and took a fighting stance near the spot where he expected the runner to emerge. Snapping twigs, thudding footsteps, labored and tremulous breathing grew louder. He spotted a shadow approaching from behind the nearest tree, so he lifted his blade and swung it.

Anieras burst from the tree line and cried out in surprise, freezing in place when he saw the sword swinging his way.

Arthur cut his swing up and away, nearly toppling over in the process to avoid beheading Anieras. The sword's wind still ruffled the long, stray wisps of silver hair atop the druid's head.

"Anieras!" Arthur snapped as he caught his balance. "Couldn't you have shouted a warning?"

The man's pale face was drenched in sweat, his eyes glassy, body shaking. His mouth moved as if to speak, but no words left his lips.

"Well?" Arthur demanded, aching from the strain of altering the course of his blade. But he took in the druid's appearance more carefully now.

"No," Anieras croaked, his voice hoarse and chest heaving with rapid breath. He held up a handful of giant, dark feathers. "It's coming."

Before Arthur could ask him for an explanation, a giant eagle let out a long, high-pitched screech from the air above, only its shadow visible through the last of the morning's lingering mist.

"Archers, ready! Spears, to me!" Arthur shouted as he sheathed his sword. There wasn't enough time to prepare a defensive formation. "Get behind me, druid!"

The eagle flapped its giant wings once, then folded them against its massive body, preparing to dive.

"Give me a spear," he ordered a nearby man, who immediately handed over his own. Arthur hefted the spear, aiming it toward the shadow as it dove through the sky.

"No!" Anieras cried out, stumbling forward and grasping Arthur's borrowed spear. "You mustn't hurt her!"

Arthur wrenched the spear away from the druid. "What do you mean? It's going to kill us!"

The bird emerged from the mist, the narrowed pupils of its enormous eyes fixed on the druid.

"Lower your weapons," the druid commanded, shouting as loudly as he could in his hoarse voice.

The respect Arthur had shown for the druid affected how much respect his warriors showed the old man, and that was never more firmly demonstrated than now. No one fired an arrow or hurled a spear; they all held steady, waiting for Arthur and whether he would give an order against the druid's. And he couldn't have been gladder about their discipline while he examined the situation. He needed more time to think, but fate had no more leniency left for him today.

The bird fully opened its wings and lowered its feet as if to land. Anieras shook so severely that Arthur worried he would bounce away into the forest again without ever taking a step. The druid shoved the feathers against Arthur's chest, and Arthur clasped them in one hand as he lowered his spear with the other.

"Take these. You must go to Calleva Atrebatum and find the golden eagle. Do whatever you must to make him your friend. Then Myrddin will need the feathers. He will help you... I..." He swallowed hard, then laid a hand briefly on Arthur's shoulder while looking him in the eyes. "Tell him I'm sorry."

Before Arthur could stop him, the druid stepped forward, arms spread wide, though he still trembled, and was immediately clutched in the talons of the gargantuan raptor. He groaned in pain as the talons squeezed his body tightly, but he didn't fight it. The downwash from the eagle's wings as it pushed upward again sent many of Arthur's people flying backward, and Arthur barely kept himself upright. He leapt forward and grasped for one of the druid's frail hands, but he was too late, and the hand was just out of reach.

He watched, helpless and confused, as the eagle rose in the air and disappeared into the mass of gray clouds far above the dissipating mist. His chest ached knowing that even if the druid freed himself, the fall would kill him.

"Anieras!" Myrddin ran to the spot where the old man had been taken from the clearing. He pulled at his hair and stared into the sky. "No, no, no!"

Arthur still clutched the feathers in one hand. He studied the deep brown color, the black patterns, incredible size and the oddly normal shape. Had this been worth the druid's life?

In his own shock, he didn't know what else to say to Myrddin. "He said these were for you."

Myrddin spun and glared at Arthur, tears streaming down his stricken face. "Feathers? I don't want your fucking feathers. I need you to save my grandfather!"

The Remnants of the Empire

ARTHUR WOULD HAVE PREFERRED to take time to mourn the loss of the druid, of a great and wise elder of his people. He didn't want to move forward so quickly, but the fate of his entire people was at stake. Time was running out for them, and the druid had offered himself up to save them.

"Should we not honor your grandfather's sacrifice and continue with the quest?"

"It's not my quest. It's yours, you arrogant bastard."

In any other scenario, Arthur would have beaten Myrddin into the ground for his impudence and very public disrespect. But the man was grieving, worried for his grandfather who'd been taken by a giant fucking eagle. The druid was probably dead now, but Arthur didn't dare speak of it.

Instead, he nodded, solemn and somber, and gestured for his wives to join him at the King Stone. To their credit, they didn't hesitate, but both women eyed the stone suspiciously and kept Arthur between it and themselves.

"We need to leave here." Arthur glanced around the clearing and the three groups of ancient stones. "How many refugees are there?"

"A dozen," Talara said. "All can walk, but most are weak or hurt."

"The girl?"

"The little one is fine. She just needed some water and a bit of food. They all need rest."

"They need to go to Caer Cadwyr," Arthur said. It was the stronghold of ancient kings, one he and his people had repaired for their habitation and protection. The last non-Roman to rule there was the leader of the Durotriges, a tribe that had disappeared well before Boudicca had razed Londinium. It had been easy to fortify and bring into repair, and there was a mystical air among the ruins that lent itself to his mission of saving his people. "Can you lead them home, Talara?"

"I'll take them," Rigana cut in. "The land crawls with Saxon vermin, and it'll take me at least three days to get them there on foot. I'll need any hands you can spare to help me."

He knew better than to argue with the fieriest of his wives over something he was likely to agree with anyway. "Take three. You choose the men."

"Should I go with you?" Talara asked, one hand on Rigana's arm.

"Nay." Rigana squeezed her hand. "Our husband will need you more than I will."

Rigana peeled off from the group to find two spearmen and one archer. All three followed her without hesitation, and they readied the refugees for the journey.

"Where will we go?" Talara asked as she eyed the King Stone, arms crossed over her chest.

"We'll go to Calleva to find the golden eagle."

"I think I've had enough of the creatures," she muttered, slinking closer to him, then tipped her head toward Myrddin crouched on the ground and sobbing quietly. "What about the bard?"

Arthur chewed his lip. "He'll have to make his own choices."

"Do you think he'll try to save Anieras?"

"How?"

She shrugged. "Surely his singing could savage the bird's ears and curdle its brain so the creature drops to the earth."

"Poor timing, my love." Arthur meant to admonish her, but he could barely hide his grin. It was terribly serious, but he realized they both needed the levity. "He will follow us if he wishes, or he'll make his own way. I don't have the time to force one man to follow the final instructions of his master. It would be folly to even try."

"Let us depart this place then. All that we can do has been done."

The way to Calleva was made easier when Arthur's party stumbled on a Roman road. Such infrastructure was a long-lasting gift from the Empire to Brittania, making their travel easier. There were a few horses, but they were used for carrying supplies. Arthur's horse, Blodwen, a flea-bitten gray mare, was well past her prime, and he only kept her from retirement to help carry the injured and the dead from battle. They'd been short on horses over the past two years. As agriculture slowed with massacres and Saxons claiming every farm they could get their hands on, food and grains grew slimmer, and livestock such as horses, oxen, cattle, and others were slaughtered for food during the hard winters.

While everyone else departed, Myrddin remained in the spot where Anieras's feet had left the earth. Arthur thought of the young man now as the road rose to a crest before him. As much as he'd wanted to stay and grieve with the young bard, he believed it was better to honor the old man's sacrifice by obeying his commands. Myrddin would have to grieve alone, as it seemed was his wish.

When Arthur topped the crest of the hill, a spring-warmed valley spread out before him, and set in it like a jewel was the great, ancient walled city of Calleva. It had been occupied for centuries before the Empire had come, but they enjoyed its location and resources so much that they'd taken it over, expanding and reinforcing the walls. They'd built baths, an amphitheater, and tall insulae for the plebians, making a modern city of it. It now stood a place of contradictions: its modern accouterments and improvements safe behind walls built centuries ago, the legendary and the common marching forward together, arm in arm.

Vibrant blue banners waved at him from the walls and through the gate, beckoning to Arthur like old friends. He hadn't been to the city since he was a child when his parents brought him on a diplomatic mission. He remembered the king of these tribes to be a stoic man, serious and somber, with a permanent frown frozen among the deeply etched lines on his worried face. Would the old ally greet Arthur as a friend now or as an enemy?

Whether the old man was still alive would probably be a better question, but Arthur didn't wish to add to the weight already bearing down on his troubled mind.

"Lanslot," he called, and the man jogged forward. "Ride down on one horse and learn whether we're welcome."

"Should I raise your banner?"

Arthur nodded, keeping his gaze on the beautiful city.

Lanslot reached for Blodwen, but Arthur raised a hand. "Not her. Find a... younger mount. And keep your shield ready."

They remained on the hill and watched as Lanslot trotted and cantered down into the valley toward Calleva, shield over his left arm, reins in his left hand, and the golden banner raised high, its pole tucked between his thigh and the horse's side. The golden banner was faded, its edges tattered, but the dark gold color still shone clear with its pale golden circle in the center. He couldn't help but feel a little tweak to his pride as he surveyed Calleva's pristine walls and crisp banners.

"How have they come out of all this so well?" Talara asked, giving voice to his thoughts.

"I'm not sure I'll like the answer."

Arthur tensed as Lanslot reached archer distance and halted, shield and banner both steady. Though Arthur was too far away to hear the conversation taking place, he watched carefully for any sign that his golden banner wouldn't be welcome in the city. But after a tense moment where horse and rider stilled to statue-like perfection, Lanslot waved the banner while circling his horse, then galloped his horse back up the road to Arthur, arriving in a few short minutes.

"They welcome Arthur, son of Uther Pendragon, and his warriors," Lanslot shouted as he approached, grinning broadly and bouncing as he slowed to a trot. "They'll open the gates to us."

"Who is king now?"

The smile slid from Lanslot's face. "I... hadn't thought to ask."

Arthur nodded. "I suppose we'll find out when we get down there then." He turned to address his people. "We must be on our best behavior. Each of you acts as a diplomat now. Any flare of temper or misstep will be severely punished. But... remain vigilant. We don't know these people or where their loyalties lie. Be prepared to defend one another and formulate an escape if we must."

Faces that shined with excitement only moments ago melted into disappointment and worry. He hated to see them like that, but he'd rather see them paranoid and on-guard than dead.

Together, they walked the road, their pace faster than it had been all day, and picking up speed when they smelled the cooking fires and heard the din of daily life rattling on behind the walls. The scent of food wafted through the air, hurrying them onward, and the nostalgia for a time of normalcy and safety ushered them further. The double-doored wooden gates were but a shadow of their Roman glory. The carvings and inscriptions honored Jupiter on one door, and Sulis-Minerva on the other. All were fading now. The skilled artisans who'd crafted and maintained them had all but disappeared after the withdrawal of Rome from Brittania. Arthur heard that upon the sacking of Rome's great capital, the Empire had retreated farther east. Artisans, crafters, and experts in architecture naturally followed the remnants of the Empire—those still with purses deep enough to commission such work.

The gates were pushed open, a giant maw inviting them all in like mice to a lion, and Arthur had to swallow the fear building in his throat before he could be tempted to turn back. To run now would show weakness and fear and would invite a fight. And if the sturdiness of this shining city was any indication, the king of Calleva had plenty of people—and likely a ready troop of soldiers. Even the guards were dressed well, an ode to Roman-Brittania. Their muted-red Roman-style tunics were worn under leather cuirasses, and uniformly beige woolen leggings snipped neatly above leather shoes. Each guard wore the Roman Galae ridge helmets that bore many dents, scrapes, and scuffs beyond simple repair.

Arthur recognized each piece, as Tintagel maintained many of the antiques. His father's armor and weapons, passed down from father to son five times since before Rome's withdrawal, was mostly seen as ceremonial, a non-functional inheritance bestowed to Arthur upon his becoming a man. The only piece of the set that Arthur used was the sword, the long spatha common to the late imperial Roman cavalry, which for him was validation of his Roman and native heritage; the latter being mixtures of Kernow and Cymry.

"I have waited too long for a visit from the son of Uther," a man with a booming voice announced as he emerged from the crowd.

Arthur halted and dipped his head lightly in respect as his warriors stopped just behind him.

"How has it come to pass that you could go nearly twenty years without visiting your cousin?"

"Cousin?"

The Golden Eagle

THE MAN WAS BROAD-SHOULDERED and thickset, tall too, though not nearly as tall as Arthur. His shoulder-length hair was mostly gray, though Arthur spotted a few flecks of blond glittering here and there. His eyes were green and piercing, intelligent and thoughtful, more like a predator's eyes than a friend's.

"Yes, Cousin Arthur! By the gods, you've grown!" He laughed and strode forward to pull Arthur into a tight hug before slapping his shoulder and drawing him forward through the clean, paved streets of Calleva. "Well, cousins through two marriages, but that counts, doesn't it? Of course it does!"

There wasn't enough space in between the man's words to allow Arthur to answer, so he kept quiet, listening and watching as they walked. He knew there was a time to speak and a time to listen, and any stranger who presumed to call him Arthur instead of Arturius was a person he needed to listen to carefully.

"I'm sure you were too young to remember when last we met—"

"Aquila?"

"Aquila Catuvellaunus, yes. I'm happy to hear you remember me, though I was a young king then and busy learning my duties and manners. We have so much to catch up on. I've sent word again and again to your parents, begging them to bring you back to Calleva, but they always come up with some reason or another to delay."

Arthur hadn't heard of any messengers bringing word from Calleva, but then again, he'd largely maintained a wide berth from court matters, much to his mother's aggravation.

"But you're here now, and we're overjoyed to greet you. What brings you to Calleva?"

The man took a breath, and Arthur took advantage of the open moment to answer before his reasons were lost to civility. "War brings me, cousin."

Nothing could be heard for several moments but the treading of their feet over the stone-paved streets as they continued forward. Arthur could feel the eyes of the people upon him, could see them in his periphery, though he kept his gaze on Aquila.

Finally, the king nodded, albeit slowly. "Come, let me show you to the forum, and we'll talk more before the grand feast tonight."

"Cousin," Arthur tossed the familiarity back at Aquila, studying his face carefully for his reaction, but the man only looked forward. "There's no need to expend a great effort on our behalf. We come as friends and, I hope, allies, not as beggars."

"If you are friends," Aquila's voice lowered, vibrating deeply with menace now, "then you will not deny our custom of hospitality to our guests."

The hairs on the back of Arthur's neck stood on end, and he suspected there was an archer or two taking aim at him from some hidden alcove high above the streets. "Of course, good King Aquila. We are your humble guests, and we would be delighted to receive your hospitality."

"There we are," Aquila said, smiling warmly as he met Arthur's gaze. "Perhaps your parents passed down their exceptional manners to you after all."

Their walk wound through busy common areas, where people stopped to watch them pass and street-side market stalls crowded the way. Arthur breathed in the mingling scents of herbs and spices, freshly baked bread, and the smoke of metalwork, glad for the moment to be in the center of so much warmth and liveliness. As they neared the forum, the modern and ancient collided, the feature for which Calleva was best known. He'd seen a well-maintained forum before in Isca Dumnoniorum, but this forum utterly dwarfed it, both in its magnificent statuary, elaborately carved columns, and friezes, as well as in its size.

Sunlight broke through the cloud cover and danced on water that trickled through a tiered series of carved stone basins at the heart of the forum. The basins featured reliefs depicting various scenes from Roman mythology, all of them centered around Jupiter, king of the Roman gods. Statues of imperial gods and long-dead emperors over-looked the scene, standing silent witness to the provincial inheritors of Roman art and architecture.

And on the left side of the throne stood a relic Arthur had heard about but never seen: a Roman standard, complete with the golden eagle crowning its faded banner.

How had Anieras known?

"Lovely, isn't it?" Aquila said quietly, his murmur almost conspir-atorial. "Wait until you see the basilica."

Arthur didn't want to leave the forum. Despite the noise of trade and commerce, the peaceful beauty of the place made him want to stay, forever lounging in splendor and opulence. As much as he wished to stay and admire the fountain with its colorful mosaic bottom,

Aquila's firm hand steered him toward a single building towering above the forum from the perimeter, the shadows of its stone arches standing in dark contrast to the pale stone exterior. Though weathered, Aquila and his ancestors had clearly done all they could to maintain the place, and their love for it shone most brightly in the interior.

Rows of elegant stone columns reached for the ceiling and worn but clean mosaics winked in the light cast by smoking braziers along the walls. At the far end of the cavernous space, King Aquila's throne sat upon a raised dais. Torches flanked the throne and cast dancing light on the colorful frescoes along the wall, reminding all onlookers of the wealth and magnificence wrought and delivered by the old Empire before its hard collapse.

Arthur wasn't usually at a loss for words, but the undeniable grandeur of the place had rendered him speechless. He wasn't stunned enough to turn a blind eye to Aquila whispering something to his guards. Those guards jogged off to usher any straggling common folk out of the building before standing at the entrance to prevent others from entering.

At least, that's what Arthur hoped they were intended to do.

"Now, cousin, we're out of the public eye. Tell me again why you've come." Aquila strode through the center of the room and sat upon his throne, back straight and strong as he looked down upon them.

"War, King Aquila," Arthur repeated. He didn't miss the significance of the man with a name that meant "eagle" sitting upon a throne with a Roman eagle as his standard.

"With whom?"

Arthur studied the man's face for a moment, sure it must have been some ruse. "The invaders. The Saxons, Angles, Jutes and all those who join them."

"And why do you bring your war to my gates?"

"I didn't think I'd have to tell you, being as close as you are to Londinium, that war will come to your gates with or without my involvement."

Aquila leaned one elbow on an armrest and tapped his chin with one finger. "What do you ask of me?"

Arthur steeled himself, quickly disciplining his tongue. "I wish to know that you are still an ally."

"An ally to whom?"

Aquila was playing games. He was no fool, and yet he insisted on making Arthur work for each and every answer. Schooling his features, Arthur fought the instinct to lash out.

"To Tintagel. To me."

"I suppose that depends. The accords signed all those years ago with your father were broken when my parents and siblings were forced to flee Londinium."

"The Saxons have taken Londinium?"

Aquila, his expression becoming grimmer, shook his head. "Not yet. But their incursions have wreaked havoc on the people. It is true—some of them come to make a better life, to live in peace with the rest of us. But the great grandsons of Hengist and Horsa have brought over legions of warriors, mercenaries without work, and they bring their sorcerers too."

Arthur thought of Anieras, wished he'd been standing there with him to give some sage and steady advice. "Do they have druids?"

"Not quite. These men and women are different. They aren't too different from the Cymry and the Kernow, I imagine, but a different... style I suppose. The darkness they bring to wage upon our people—"

"We've seen it already. They're burning the towns and villages, cutting down our people. It's wanton killing and destruction beyond these walls, King."

Aquila nodded. "I'm well aware, Arthur. They're not like the others who are simply looking for their own plot of land to farm and livestock to raise. They're killing the animals and leaving the bodies to rot, burning fields to ash."

"If you know all this, then why do you feign ignorance at my presence?"

"Because," Aquila said through clenched teeth, his voice low, "no one came to my aid when they came for my parents, my brothers, my sisters."

"Word did not reach us, and I give you my utmost regret at those you've lost."

"My parents..." He ground his teeth, then relaxed his jaw a fraction. "They didn't make it. My sisters did, and two of my four brothers. Although they're here now, what they saw changed them. I'm always the one left to pick up the pieces when things are broken, when trust is broken."

"And what could I possibly do to rebuild the trust and alliance between us?"

Aquila's grimace softened and turned into a satisfied grin. "Now that you bring it up—in your brash and graceless manner—I know of only one thing that would restore the bond between our families."

"Anything, King Aquila," Arthur said, hating the open promise but unable to ignore the golden eagle sitting atop the standard next to the throne. Anieras had made it unquestionably clear that the first part of his quest was to befriend the golden eagle. He'd sacrificed himself to gain clarity on that part of Anieras's vision and to gather what they needed for the next part—if Myrddin returned to them and fulfilled his role.

"Anything?" The king quirked an eyebrow.

"I swear it upon the old gods and the new."

Aquila tapped the arm of his throne with one fingertip, as if deep in contemplation.

"I will bind my oath in blood," Arthur offered.

The king raised a hand and shook his head. "Please don't spill blood in my basilica. It's difficult to clean, and I don't have the skilled men needed to replace the tiles if you stain them. I'll take you at your word, young king. I strongly advise you not to break it."

Arthur swallowed the dread that welled up within him and nodded his head firmly. He could only beg the gods that the odd king Aquila wouldn't force him to kill any of his warriors or... Talara. The thought of something happening to his beloved wife made his stomach swirl and his heart beat faster, but he said nothing and kept his clenched fists at his sides as he waited for the king to complete this cat-and-mouse game.

Aquila rose to his feet and motioned to someone standing in an entrance shrouded in shadows. Arthur was stunned that he hadn't noticed the entrance or the person, so he watched intently to see who had escaped his notice.

A maiden with long, pale golden hair walked into the light and approached the dais. She wore an impossibly white dress, and he watched transfixed as she knelt beside the throne and bowed her head. As young and beautiful and mesmerizing as she was, Arthur couldn't help but feel something bad was about to happen, and his open promise would have to be broken. And if that happened, would he and his people be allowed to leave Calleva unscathed? He resisted the urge to draw his sword, waiting with bated breath for the golden eagle to name his demands.

"Rise, sister, and meet your husband-to-be."

"Arthur, this is Gwynafar."

Drink the Wine

ARTHUR BEGAN TO SWEAT as the woman approached him. In a silent, graceful motion, she almost imperceptibly lifted the hem of her dress, to lift it off the floor, and bowed to him.

"Arthur," she said, lifting her ice-blue eyes to meet his. The curve of her soft red lips and the blush on her cheeks told Arthur she wasn't unhappy with the match. "You may not remember me. I was a little girl when you visited, but we played together in the gardens."

A distant memory struck him, and it was as if he could see it then: he and a little blonde girl playing among flowers and trees. It was only a few faint flashes, but they were brought to the surface, nonetheless.

"I remember," he responded, trying to sound firm but altogether failing. "It is nice to see you again."

She smiled, her eyes glittering as she stared up at him.

"Ah! It is love!" King Aquila declared, laughing easily.

Arthur shook his head and turned his attention back to Aquila. "I apologize if no one has told you, King Aquila, but I am already married."

Aquila's laughter stopped abruptly, and he dropped onto his throne. "Already married?"

"I am. But if there is anything else I may do to restore our—"

"There's nothing wrong with having two wives." Aquila's tone had turned sour.

"I already have two wives." Arthur smiled, amused that Aquila hadn't known. "What could I possibly want with a third wife?"

Aquila did not find it as amusing as Arthur did, and his frown turned into a grimace. "You made a promise, Arturius."

The use of Arthur's formal name stole any warmth or amusement from him, but he didn't feel fear. He was aching for a fight. He didn't like being jerked around, and he didn't have the time for it. He dropped the pretenses, laughed grimly—more out of exhaustion than poor humor—and rubbed the bridge of his nose with one hand. "Blood is being spilt outside these walls, and every minute we waste here with this ridiculous game could be yet another life lost to the invaders. What kind of king waits on the sidelines and arranges marriages instead of riding out into battle?"

A familiar hand rested gently on his shoulder—Talara, he knew instinctively—as Gwynafar's gaze shifted to someone standing just behind Arthur and to his side. The fair maiden's pleasant smile melted, and her gentle eyes turned hard as she backed away from him. She returned to the dais and stood by her brother's throne as he fumed, red-faced and speechless.

"And what man dares disrespect a king in his own hall?" he finally thundered, his voice echoing in the room.

Arthur heard the ring of blades being unsheathed and the clinking of armor behind him, and he knew he'd stepped too far. He raised a hand just above his shoulder and clenched his fist. "Steady. These people are not our enemies."

"Brave words from a brash young king," Aquila spat, slamming a fist on the armrest.

"Why does everyone keep calling me that? I'm not a king!"

"But aren't you?" It was Gwynafar who spoke up this time, her voice as soft as a gently flowing river on a summer's eve. She arched a golden eyebrow and stood politely next to Aquila's throne, the light of the room seeming to collect around her.

Arthur blinked rapidly, trying to clear his vision. "No. My father is king at Tintagel, my mother is the queen. But should I ever return and be deemed fit to rule, then I may be called a king."

"You are the king at Caer Cadwyr, are you not?" Aquila challenged.

"I've taken no such title."

"What do they call you then?"

"They call me Arturius. And the druid," he swallowed the tightness in his throat that came with remembering Anieras, "calls me Dux Bellorum. My friends call me leader, and my enemies call me slayer. There are many names and titles bestowed upon me, and I care for none but my name. The only question that remains now is what *you* will call me, King of Calleva? Ally," he tapped the hilt of his spatha with one hand, "or enemy?"

Aquila burst up from his chair, and everyone seemed to jump except Arthur. He stood still as a statue as the king stormed down from the dais and straight for him, eyes locked on the king and his body pumping with adrenaline. If he'd been hoping to intimidate Arthur, he was failing.

The king stopped in front of Arthur, eyes locked in a war for dominance, but he was already losing. Arthur looked down at the king, and he saw fear in him. There was a secret behind those eyes, one that Arthur knew he needed to unlock.

Aquila's eyes softened, and he smiled before taking a deep breath and speaking loud enough for everyone to hear. "I will not call you the enemy."

He held out his arm, but Arthur didn't take it immediately.

"But," the king continued, more softly now, "I will not call you my ally unless you marry my sister. We must be bonded through marriage and through blood."

Do whatever you must to make him your friend. It was Anieras's voice ringing in his head as he weighed his choices. He found it hard to believe that a creature of legend had snatched the man off his feet only that morning.

Arthur nodded and clasped the man's arm. "If that is your greatest need of me, then I will marry her."

Arthur was not surprised to find that the feast Aquila planned had been a wedding feast all along. Without the druid, Arthur might have found his way out of this mess. Instead, he'd surrendered to the threads fate had spun for him. He sat next to his new bride near the king at the head of a long table arranged in the center of the basilica. Many of Calleva's prominent families sat at the table, with Aquila's relatives sitting closest to him. Arthur's warriors were all given seats at the table, and he was silently thankful he hadn't needed to insist on places for the few women among his group. Talara, sitting on his other side, had been cold and quiet since he agreed to marry Gwynafar, but he hadn't yet found the opportunity to pull her aside and speak privately.

"Have you tried the mead?" he asked, turning and whispering in his second wife's ear.

She nodded, then put the cup to her lips, holding his gaze as she drank. "It's a fine mead."

He reached down to lovingly squeeze her thigh under the table, but Gwynafar decided at that moment to pull his face to hers and kiss him. The surrounding crowd hollered and cheered, and Talara roughly pushed his hand away.

"Damn it," he muttered under his breath when Gwynafar finally pulled away.

She blushed deeply, her eyes glassy from her overindulgence in the mead. With a broad smile, she stared into his eyes, hers wide and playful, or so it seemed. His mind felt fuzzy as she beamed at him. There was something false about the air of girlish innocence she put on, and he hoped that was the only reason Talara now gave him the cold shoulder.

All the food served seemed an overt demonstration of the city's abundance and prosperity. The table overflowed with herbed breads, honey cakes, roast pork and venison, smoked trout, cheeses, herb-roasted lentils, mead, and ale. His bride was only a few years younger than he, and he was surprised she'd reached the age of twenty and two years without already being married off.

As the ale loosened Arthur's tongue, he raised the question to his new brother-in-law. "Why did you wait so long to have her married?"

Aquila's laugh boomed through the hall, sharp even above the rumble of conversation. "You never read the accords your parents signed, did you?"

Arthur shook his head and finished his cup. As soon as it touched the table, a serving girl filled it again.

"To seal our alliance, it was promised that Calleva and Tintagel would be united through marriage. One Catuvellaunus and one Pendragon must be wed." The king squeezed his sister's hand, and she squeezed his in return. "After nearly two damned decades, that promise is finally fulfilled."

"Husband," Gwynafar started.

The word grated on Arthur, and he couldn't resist a grimace. He kept his words simple, feeling Talara's gaze burning into the back of his skull. "Yes?"

"How long will we stay in Calleva?"

"Unless your brother has any other need of me, we must be on our way as early as possible." It was true, even if he didn't know exactly where they'd be going next. He hoped that in Myrddin's absence, one of the gods would offer some hint.

"I have no need but to share with my new brother!" Aquila declared, his cheeks flushed from drinking. He'd had a drink of everything the serving girls had brought out and had been deep in his cups before the impromptu wedding had even finished. The glass and Samian wares had to be replaced with wooden cups before the feast had even begun.

Arthur tried not to let his want show. "What will my newest brother share with me?"

He put on his widest smile and raised his cup to Aquila. The king couldn't resist the opportunity to smash his wooden cup against Arthur's, grinning with simple pleasure.

"Weapons, armor, food." He spread his arm at the table. "What else do you need?"

Arthur thought for a moment, looking around to give the appearance of contemplation, though he didn't need it. "Horses."

"Then the great Dux Bellorum—my new brother—will have the bloody horses!" His laughter rippled like thunder over the noise of the hall. Arthur laughed with him, but he let the smaller man be louder. He'd give him that deference if he could have all his warriors mounted.

Talara remained cold to him, though she laughed, drank, and sang with the surrounding warriors, and he supposed he'd have to endure it until she could contain her words no longer.

Aquila grabbed at a passing woman. She couldn't dodge him, but she kept her pitcher steady, and not a drop spilled as he pulled her into his lap. "Pour me a drink, lovely woman."

Arthur turned to his new bride. Her gaze was fixed on something across the table, so he followed it. Their relatives sat along the other side of the table, but it wasn't them she was staring at. Those piercing eyes were focused on Lanslot standing at a distance behind them. Arthur's old friend was talking with a guard, surely comparing swords or whipping up war stories.

If Gwynafar noticed Arthur glancing between her and Lanslot, she pretended not to.

Heat crawled up his neck, and he raised his cup in front of a woman passing by with a pitcher in hand.

"It's wine," she said, her eyes sliding down, then back up again. She grinned. "But it's the best wine you'll find tonight."

Arthur smiled, warmer now, their eyes locked as she poured the red liquid into his cup.

Gwynafar turned slowly in her seat, looked between the two of them, then slapped the cup out of Arthur's hand. Wine splashed across the guests down the table from him, and the cup hit Talara in the back of the head.

"Poison!" Gwynafar jumped up with such force that her chair fell backward. She raised one delicate arm and pointed a pale finger at the serving woman who stood frozen, staring wide-eyed at the king's sister. "Guards!"

Men rushed forward through the crowd of people, and the serving woman spun in a circle. The ceramic pitcher fell from her hands and shattered on the floor, and the tang of red wine filled the air. Seeing men with drawn swords surrounding her, she cried and dropped to her knees at Gwynafar's feet.

"Please, lady! I beg your mercy! There is no poison. I swear it on my life!"

Gwynafar's cold eyes stared down at the woman's crouched form, glaring as if she could impale her with a look. But then Arthur knew she could. One knowing look to the guards, and the poor woman would be executed.

"I don't believe you," she whispered, her warm lips in harsh contrast to the cold of her expressionless face. "You wanted to murder my husband."

Aquila, who'd been distracted with his own serving woman, finally spoke up. "Take this woman—"

"No," Arthur said firmly as he rose and wiped the wine from his face. "There is no poison."

His new wife turned that icy stare on him, slow and careful. "My King—"

"Not a king," he corrected, his face hot with embarrassment as every eye in the hall turned to them.

"My lord, I understand that you have enjoyed our great city's hospitality today, but you do not understand the dangers as well as we do. I know a poisoner—"

"Lanslot," Arthur barked, and the man came running.

"Yes, Arturius," he answered, pushing without hesitation through the crowd of guards, his signature charming smile never leaving his face.

"See that cup?" Arthur pointed to his cup lying on the floor. "Pick it up and drink any wine that may be left in it."

Lanslot looked at the cup, then back at Arthur. "You're sure?"

Arthur nodded, then turned back to his wife. "Those who follow me will do anything for our quest. Even if it means dying. Do you know what our quest is, lady?"

Her eyes narrowed, lips pursed, almost imperceptibly, but Arthur caught them. They both knew her measure then.

"Our quest is to save our people and our way of life from the invaders. If we go about killing those of our people by whom we feel offended, then we might as well save our strength and let the Saxons slaughter us in our homes. Well, the men anyway. Do you know what they like to do to our women?"

Her eyes widened ever so slightly, and he knew he had her right where he wanted her. A pressure filled his head as the air between them shimmered, but he ignored it, sure it was the abundance of wine that now tricked his eyes and needled at his brain.

"And to the wives of war chiefs..." He tsked and shook his head. "Talara. Tell your new hearth-sister what awaits her outside those walls."

Gywnafar turned absolutely pale, and her perfect lips parted, though no sound passed them.

"Brother," Aquila interjected, his tone conciliatory. "There's no need to—"

"Lanslot, drink the wine." Arthur never took his focus from Gwynafar's face, though her gaze flickered to Lanslot.

To his credit, his friend did not hesitate again. He bent, lifted the cup to his lips, and tossed back the small splash of liquid that remained.

Arthur's newest wife didn't so much as flinch.

A Different Kind of Battle

Lanslot didn't smile after he licked the last drop of wine from his lips. He waited, clearly as nervous as everyone else. The air in the basilica was tense, and the cavernous room so quiet they could hear the crackle of the torches burning.

"I feel fine," he said, shrugging as he held the cup forward. "I could go for another."

Gwynafar glared at Arthur.

"It seems you were wrong about the poison," Arthur said, putting on a soft smile he didn't feel. The small pressure in his head swelled into a sharp throbbing sensation.

The crowd seemed to give a collective sigh of relief. Conversation started once again, a murmur at first, but it quickly returned to its previous raucous fervor.

Gwynafar viciously kicked the woman off of her and stepped close to Arthur. She wrapped her arms around his neck and leaned up on her tiptoes, never taking her hard eyes from his. "You'll soon learn that I'm never wrong, husband."

He rested his hands on her slender hips and leaned forward. She softened as if expecting a kiss, but he moved her aside. Leaning down, he ignored the fuming beauty, gritted his teeth against the pounding in his head, and lifted the shaking server woman from the floor. "Are you hurt, good lady?"

Arthur hoped Gwynafar had heard his emphasis on "good" and "lady."

The woman moved gingerly, but nodded.

"Please, take my seat. And if anyone has a problem with it," he gave pointed looks at everyone around them, "they can answer to me."

He motioned for someone to bring her a drink, then wandered away from the table to mingle with the guests. He quickly found Lanslot, happily drinking more wine. He clapped Arthur's shoulder and pulled him into the circle of warriors that had gathered around him.

"But for all my victories, they pale compared to those of Arturius, my friend and my war chief."

"Don't let him deceive you," Arthur said, waving off his friend's bragging. "Walk with me."

Lanslot excused them from the group, and they left the basilica and strolled out into the forum.

The night air still carried the edge of winter, but Arthur gratefully sucked in the cold air as the noise of the feast faded.

"What was that all about?"

"That woman," Arthur grumbled, walking to the fountain. He dipped a hand into the nearest of the stone basins and traced his fingers along the top of the water. "Nothing but trouble even before I met her."

"Try to think of how she might feel, Arthur. She's been forced to marry a man she doesn't know, one who already has two wives. She's young. She's scared."

Arthur laughed and splashed water on his face. "She's not that young. And I don't believe for a second that she's scared. That woman is a—"

"Which woman?" Talara asked as she came up behind them.

"I suppose that could apply to either of you." Lanslot laughed and splashed a handful of icy water at her.

"How old are you?" she asked, voice thick with scorn.

"Not as old as—"

Talara took one quick stride into Lanslot's space, hooked a foot behind his ankle, and pushed him backward into the lowest of the stone basins. He yelped, then gasped at the shock of the freezing water. The basin wasn't deep enough to drown him, but he struggled to push himself up, and to unhook the backs of his knees from the edge.

"There's my strong and beautiful wife," Arthur said, offering his hand.

She looked at his hand, then at his eyes, and sighed before taking it. "I'm still angry."

"Why are you angry with me?"

"Not at you. Well, maybe a little. I simply... I don't like this place," she whispered, gesturing around them. "And I don't like those people. Something's not right. Everything seems beautiful, but something lurks beneath this veil."

"I didn't want any of this. I'm just—"

"I know." She sighed, pushing Lanslot back in the water just as he pulled himself out, then hugged Arthur. "We need to leave. We've befriended your golden eagle. Let's go."

"Brother!"

Arthur groaned inwardly and rolled his eyes as he listened to Aquila's approaching footsteps.

"I understand you have a wife in your arms currently, but your newest requires your attention on your wedding night. You need children. Immediately!"

"Talara, please—"

"Help me, you witch!" Lanslot called, voice shaking with cold.

She squeezed Arthur's hands, stepped back, and lent her arm to Lanslot to help him from the water.

"Go," she ordered him, waving a hand toward the basilica. "Perhaps having a husband will transform her into a more pleasant person." Talara glanced at Aquila. "I mean no offense, Lord."

"You'll hear no objection from me." He winked, laughed, and burped, nearly all at once.

Talara shot Arthur an annoyed look and walked away.

He sighed deeply, then headed back into the basilica to find his third—and most troublesome—wife.

Horses chewed their breakfast as Arthur walked through the stable with his closest companions, Talara among them. Occasionally, he would nod toward a horse, and someone would collect it, saddle it, and add it to their herd. Drystan kept a tally of the number of horses needed, including a few in case of injuries, and ticked them off as they went.

When Talara had gone ahead to preview a few more horses, Drystan slowed with Arthur and nudged him with an elbow. "How was last night?"

Arthur scoffed and shook his head. "Miserable."

"No!" He looked around for Talara, made sure they weren't within earshot before continuing. "Not with that beauty."

"I'm wondering if there was a very good reason why my parents didn't tell me about the accords and their inclusion of a marriage contract."

"Come now, old friend. You've claimed women as hard, fierce, and wild as Rigana and Talara as wives, but this new, fragile, sheltered woman is beyond your ability to tame?"

Arthur stopped, caught Drystan's gaze, and shook his head firmly. "Know this: my first two wives are not by any means 'tamed'. I'm fortunate they like me, let alone love me as much as they do. Gwynafar does not like me, and I doubt she'll love me."

"Bah!" Drystan slapped his shoulder. "Give it time. She'll come to love you as much as everyone does."

"Some things you know right away. I'll never desire her love." Arthur glanced at Talara, her black braided hair swinging at the small of her back as she rubbed the face of a blood bay horse. "I only needed her brother as my ally, and that was his one requirement."

That fact stuck out to Arthur as he thought it over, but the day was burning away, and he didn't have time to delve into another worry.

"What is our next destination?"

"I was told to welcome the siren."

"But..." Drystan pushed.

"Myrddin was supposed to tell us where we would go."

"Should we find him?"

Arthur shook his head. "No. If it is destined, he will find us. I..." He swallowed hard as he remembered the dark vision of water and land that had swirled behind his eyes in the place between consciousness and sleep. "I had a dream last night about Ynis Witrin."

Whatever joke had been sitting on the tip of Drystan's tongue died with the amusement in his eyes.

"We will make an offering to *Mars Rigisamus* to confirm my vision, and then we will follow whatever sign he sends. The gods are with us, Drystan."

His friend said nothing more, but the creases between his brows betrayed his worry.

Arthur caught up with their escort. "Magister Equitum, does my new wife have a favorite horse?"

The man nodded. "Yes, Dux Bellorum, she does." He hurried up a few stalls and gestured inside.

A magnificent white horse chewed away at its roughage, unconcerned with their presence. "It's a mare?"

"Draegan is a gelding, Dux Bellorum."

Arthur winced. "Why give him a name like that and geld him?"

The master of horses stared back at him, unblinking, but he didn't answer.

"Please ready him." Arthur sighed and walked on.

"I will prepare the carrus, Dux Bellorum."

Arthur froze. "*Carrus*?"

"It is lovely, as you'll see, and worthy of your new bride, I promise. I'm sure your other wife will also enjoy it."

Talara turned swiftly, eyes narrowing and flicking between the master of horses and Arthur.

"Follow me." The man led them through a passageway to a separate area of the building that housed various riding and cavalry implements, and many wagons and chariots. He stopped at the very end of a long line of wagons and pointed. The two-wheeled carrus had a wooden structure covered with a roof and sides of leather and lavished in bright purple cloth. Any wood not covered was elaborately carved with old Roman motifs and scenes from the birth of Venus.

He pulled back a yellow braided rope to show the interior of the carrus, covered in plush cushions, soft furs, and colorful cloth draped over the broad windows.

"No." Arthur waved a hand at the master of horses. "Gwynafar will ride. Our quest requires speed, stamina, and the ability to go where wagons cannot. We will most often be off the roads."

The man looked horrified. "Dux Bellorum, you have my greatest respect, but..."

"Yes?"

"But the king's sister does not ride on a horse; she rides only in her carrus."

Arthur ground his teeth. "I'm telling you now, she will ride on her horse. There is no other option."

He looked about to argue but then closed his mouth, closed the carrus, and bowed slightly. "Of course, Dux Bellorum. But—"

"What?" Arthur snapped.

"Draegan is unfit for long travel. He is conditioned for short trips only and is used to pull the carrus rather than carry a rider."

"Her preferred horse is not suitable then."

The master of horses shook his head.

"So find her a horse that is suitable," Arthur ordered. "Preferably a well-fed one that's easier for her to ride. Have it saddled and ready with the rest of them. Talara, Drystan. Finish without me."

Arthur stalked out of the well-maintained Roman stables and headed to the basilica. When he entered, he found King Aquila, Gwynafar, and a small group enjoying a morning meal. Their conversation burbled with laughter and hushed words, but as soon as his footsteps echoed across the tiles, all fell silent.

He'd made the mistake of thinking he couldn't be any more aggravated with Gwynafar after seeing her carrus. Now, she was laughing over breakfast with her closest friends, and he was probably the butt of their joke. Heat climbed up his neck and burned his ears as he approached the table.

He stopped when he neared it and dipped his head sharply to King Aquila. "Good morning."

"It's a beautiful morning, isn't it, brother?" The king's cheeks were flushed, and the scent of mead wafted up to Arthur.

"It is. I wanted to thank you for your gracious hospitality, for the alliance we've forged, and for the aid you have given us in weapons, horses, and supplies." Arthur hoped his failure to mention Gwynafar would be easily missed.

The delighted grin she'd had before she noticed him had melted into a tight-lipped smile that didn't reach her eyes, but she said nothing.

"Of course, brother. We are family now, after all. I'll provide all you need to keep you, and especially the youngest of my sisters, safe as you rid our land of the Saxon invaders."

Before Arthur could answer, Gwynafar interjected. "We shall leave for Tintagel in, perhaps, a month or two?"

He hoped she couldn't seriously be that oblivious, or that stubborn.

"We're not going to Tintagel."

"What? Caer Cadwyr, then? In two months' time, of course."

He shook his head, neck burning hotter from frustration than embarrassment now.

"No," he said, keeping his voice soft. She had a passive way of pressing her desires upon others, but Tintagel was at least a week's ride, especially with his full warband, and he had no intention of delaying his quest to cater to the vapid wants of this woman.

She laughed in that airy, light voice, as if it was a game, but Arthur knew he was now in a battle of a different kind. "Will you send me with your soldiers then?"

"No. I will need every man and woman I have. I've already lost four to the escort of refugees to Caer Cadwyr."

She pouted her lower lip, her eyes wide and innocent. "When will we return to Tintagel, beloved?"

Arthur met Aquila's gaze, and the man shrugged.

"We will not go to Tintagel."

"Oh? Where then, husband?"

Gwynafar raised a ceramic cup to her smiling mouth, her pale eyes offering only contempt and challenge.

"We shall travel to Ynys Witrin. As I made clear yesterday, we cannot delay."

She choked on her mint tea, eyes wide as she looked around the table. Composing herself, she gently set down her cup and dabbed her mouth delicately with her mappa. "By Ynys Witrin, you mean Insula Avallonis?"

Arthur saw the fear in her eyes, and he tried not to grin too broadly. "Indeed. I'm happy to see you've heard of it."

"It's a swamp," she declared, laughing derisively as she looked around at her breakfast companions for validation.

The women sipped from their cups, and the men ate their food, but no one joined in her laughter.

"Brother," Aquila said, then forced a soft chuckle. "Surely you cannot mean to take my sister into the marshlands. It isn't safe—"

"Brother, I will be frank with you. I refuse to stray from my quest simply to seat your sister on a golden cushion somewhere so she can

plague my family or my people with her quick temper and false alle-
gations."

The entire table fell silent, frozen by Arthur's brash charge. It was
Gwynafar's turn to be red in the face.

"If you believe that she's safer here, then she can stay with you while
I go out beyond the walls and fight with every piece of my soul to save
our people." Arthur enjoyed standing up for himself and his people,
and his chest swelled with confidence and pride once more. He was
also eager to be rid of the unbearable woman.

"Husband," Gwynafar spoke before her brother could, rising from
her seat and walking to him. She placed both hands on one of his arms,
her touch warm and light as a feather. "Please do not speak so poorly
of me. I know you are unhappy about last night, but I only did what
I thought a wife should do. I was worried for your safety, my love."

There were tears in her eyes now, glistening at the corners, and her
words almost moved him. Almost.

"You are the savior of our people, the great warlord, and I will stand
with you every step of the way if you'll only give me the chance. But if
I would be in the way, then I shall remain here at Calleva until you are
ready to bring me to my new home in—"

"No!" Aquila barked, then let out another of those annoying
chuckles. "I mean, no, sister. A wife should be with her husband, and
she should share in his trials and hardships."

"What?" Arthur and Gwynafar replied together, then glanced at
each other.

"And who better to protect her than her husband? Besides, you two
need to make a child to produce an heir, Arturius!"

Arthur resisted the urge to glower at the man. Neither of them
wanted to deal with Her Grace, the royal pain in the ass.

Or was it something more?

"Where we're heading, there will be little time for such pursuits," Arthur said firmly.

"Please, Aquila," she pleaded, turning to him with those big doe eyes. "I shan't burden my husband's noble mission."

His jaw clenched, he stared at his sister with glassy eyes. He finished his mead in one swig and slammed the wooden cup on the table. "It is settled, Gwynafar."

She looked relieved for a moment, the softest, truest smile gracing her lips, but Aquila wasn't finished speaking.

"You will join your husband."

Bound and Gagged and Thrown on the Back of a Horse

The offering to Mars Rigisamus had been prepared while Arthur was failing to convince Aquila to keep his sister. Once the hall was cleared of Aquila's meal, the warband joined Arthur in the now quiet basilica. The altar to the Roman Mars already held offerings of fruit, feathers, and trinkets, and the surrounding air was heavy with anticipation of the ritual. Though the statue watching over them honored the god of war in his Roman form, the offerings and ritual were meant for Rigisamus. Drystan lit a fire in the altar's brazier, dark coals glowing beneath the flames, and Talara carried a bundle of wild sage in one hand. Everyone held their helmets under their left arm.

Talara, once a student of the druids until her marriage to Arthur, led the ritual. She was first to lay her helmet at the base of the altar, and each member of the warband followed suit. Gwynafar approached last, just after Arthur. She hesitated, then removed one of her many rings and placed it among the helmets. Talara tossed the bundle of sage into the fire and raised her arms, palms skyward. She spoke ably in the secret language of the druids, calling on the god of war, asking Mars Rigisamus to bless their quest and to give them a sign that going to Ynys Witrin was the correct path.

Arthur closed his eyes and listened, drinking in the words as she spoke, and giving his spirit over to the ritual. The heaviness in the air lifted as a light breeze swept in from the entrance, stirring his hair and brushing his cheek. It reminded him of the kiss of the Morrigan, and he could feel the lingering ice where her lips had chilled his skin. He wasn't afraid; she hadn't left him with such a feeling. Only a feeling of gratitude for her blessing returned with the memory.

After Talara finished the prayer, she clasped her hands together, squeezed her eyes tightly shut, and sang unfamiliar words in the secret tongue.

The breeze died as she sang, and Arthur felt his skin warm. The sensation started gently, then grew in intensity. His fingers ached for the cold steel of his blade, but he resisted. He opened his eyes and stared into the fire burning at the altar of Mars. Figures danced in the flames, swinging, stabbing, impaling each other. They fell away, and new ones rose, their little orange and yellow bodies dancing in the blood of their enemies. Then the flames swirled, and a dragon stalked toward the victors, chomping them up in its jaws and ripping them apart with its long talons.

Arthur wanted to jump and shout to the others what he had seen, but he was frozen, enchanted as the scenes played out on the bed of coals. The dragon fell and its victims fell away, and a feminine body of orange and yellow rose in its place, long swirls of hair flying behind her. She pointed one hand, and he followed its path to find a great mountain with a lake at its foot. It seemed important in its magnifi-cence, like something he should recognize, a name teasing the tip of his tongue. The mountain's snowy top glared at him from within the flames, and the waves on the lake glittered coldly, blinding him with their brightness.

The pitch of Talara's song changed, and Arthur could feel the bodies of his soldiers swaying around him. Still, he couldn't tear his gaze from the flames. The mountain flickered away, and he saw a great hill surrounded by marshland. A circle of stone and wooden columns topped the hill, and people danced around a blazing fire in the center. Moonlight reflected on the calm, inky surface of a river winding through a valley stretching beyond the hill and its dancers.

Long, slender fingers broke the surface, then curled and waved, beckoning Arthur forward. Compelled by the figure in flame, he took one step closer to the fire. He'd have taken another, but someone grabbed his arm, and it shook him from the spell. Gone were the images of the hill, the river, the delicate hand.

"Here," Drystan whispered, handing him a pitcher.

Arthur accepted it and found the pungent scent of the deep red wine almost overwhelming.

Talara opened her eyes and unclasped her hands before turning to Arthur. He handed her the pitcher of wine, and she faced the fire before pouring a healthy serving into it, whispering words under her breath as the coals popped and the flames danced. The wine evaporated and its heavy scent permeated the surrounding air, at once both fragrant and smoky.

"Thanks be to Mars Rigisamus!" she cried, her strong, clear, beautiful voice echoing through the basilica.

"Thanks be to Mars Rigisamus!" the warband shouted after her, their collective voice thundering in the space.

"Thanks be to Mars Rigisamus," Gwynafar said softly, her words just behind the rest of the group's.

"No, husband. You shan't force me to ride horseback! I'm a noble lady, and I must ride in my carrus."

Arthur clenched his fists and stalked toward her. "I've seen your carrus, and all this luxury to which you've become so accustomed. But it is not fit for our travels. You will ride horseback on the horse chosen for you—"

"The only horse I'll ride is Draegan—"

"If you want to kill your beloved horse, then by all means, we'll bring him."

Her mouth snapped shut like a trap.

"Now, here's the horse that we've selected for you."

She looked at the muscular sorrel horse with its cropped mane and grimaced. "I refuse to ride that ugly thing, and no amount of shouting and embarrassing me in front of your soldiers is going to make me do it."

Her words slammed against his brain, but the vicious pain from the previous day was now muted, the throbbing sensation less stabbing and more muffled to his senses. He leaned in close until their noses nearly touched, and they locked eyes as he growled in a low whisper. "You will ride that magnificent steed, or I will tie your hands and feet and throw you over the ass of my horse. One more word against me, and I'll have you gagged."

"Ah, the joys and pains of marriage," Aquila observed with a laugh from nearby. "The lovebirds will have their quarrels, but it is true love that finds compromise amid such trials."

"Mount the horse," Arthur commanded through clenched teeth.

Gwynafar's bottom lip quivered, and her eyes welled with tears.

He kept his voice low and wagged a finger at her. "If you cry, you will be bound and gagged and thrown on the back of my horse."

Her lip stopped quivering, and her eyes turned steely. "And how shall I do that in my skirts? Do you wish me to show my legs to your men?" She shot a glare at Talara standing nearby with the blood bay mare. "Or perhaps your other wives like women."

Arthur shot a hand forward and grabbed her firmly by the jaw. "Speak one more word against either of your hearth sisters and riding on the ass of my horse will be the least of your troubles."

She shook herself from his grasp and pulled backward before letting out a muffled shriek and stomping a foot. "Fine. I'll show my legs to your—"

A pair of woolen trousers smacked her softly in the face, followed by, "Catch this!" from Talara.

She turned slowly and glared at Talara, but Arthur's second wife only smiled and waved, then lifted the hem of her tunic a little to show off her own trousers. "They're warm, and they're more comfortable to ride in than a skirt."

Gwynafar turned back to Arthur, shooting him daggers the entire time as she picked up the trousers and bent over to pass them under the skirt of her dress and pull them on. Her waist-length blonde hair fell over her shoulder as she struggled into the trousers, and as unbalanced as she was, she never took her fierce gaze off Arthur.

Learning from Talara's example, Arthur smiled. He turned to his new brother-in-law and slapped him on the shoulder. "Your hospitality is unmatched, King Aquila. You have given me quite the little prize to bring along on my journey."

She froze at that, staring up at him with a slack jaw. Wobbling, she fell to the ground, and everyone laughed, though most tried to muffle it.

"Gwyn! You're drunk again!" Aquila said through his own laughter as Arthur moved to help her up.

Once she was on her feet, she gripped his arm with one hand to steady herself and used the other to finish awkwardly pulling up the trousers. She pushed him away when she had them on and stomped toward her horse.

"His name is Caius," Arthur said as he helped her up onto the horse's back.

Gwynafar settled herself, her lips pursed, then picked up the reins and tapped her heels into the stallion's sides.

"It seems she's as ready to get on with your quest as you are." Aquila laughed. "Farewell, Gwynafar. We'll meet again soon, little sister."

"Brother," Arthur said, holding out his sword arm to the king.

Aquila pulled him in for a manly hug, clapping Arthur on the shoulder before letting him go. He smelled like he'd fallen in a mead barrel, and his eyes had a glazed look.

"You'll be all right?" Arthur asked, suddenly worried for the man, though he couldn't imagine why after being strong-armed into an unhappy marriage.

"Aye." Aquila nodded, glancing toward his sister as she neared the north gate of Calleva. "We'll be fine here. Our walls are strong, our gate narrow, and our trenches deep."

"They are. You are well-protected. I'll be glad to return to you with news of our quest. Thank you again for the supplies."

"I have one more parting gift for you, Arturius."

He sounded so serious that Arthur straightened, watching intently as one of Aquila's personal guardsmen came forward holding a Roman standard. The lightly faded red and gold banner fluttered in the morning air, but the golden eagle atop it still glinted in the morning light.

"This is too generous a gift. I couldn't—"

"You must carry the eagle, Dux Bellorum. You are leading our people into battle. This is not the standard in my hall, but one kept safe by my family over the years." He took the standard from the guard, then held it forward to Arthur. "And know that after your quest is completed, when the time comes for great courage, my standard will join yours on the battlefield."

Arthur accepted the standard, grasping the reworked wooden pole in his hands, the golden eagle hovering over him like a vigilant spirit.

"Any final advice for how I should make the best of things with your sister?"

Aquila froze, almost imperceptibly, but Arthur swore it was fear burning there in the man's eyes. He shook his head and put on a smile. "Remember that marriages aren't always joyous things, Arthur. You are lucky in your first two. My two wives—both now awaiting me in Annwn—came to an understanding with me. They declared their needs, and I declared my own. We found our common ground and understood our duty to our people. I hope you and Gwyn can do the same."

"I'll treat her as well as she'll let me," Arthur said, and he meant it.

Aquila snorted. "She'll make your life miserable if you don't. My advice? Give her a little something each day, some surprise. Could be a trinket, a gift, food, or simply doing something she doesn't expect for her. That usually keeps her temper at bay."

Arthur waved a hand dismissively. "Her temper isn't all that bad. It's just aggravating. What's a twig like that going to do anyway?"

Aquila looked him in the eye, all the mirth drained from his mead-blushed face. "Oh, that incident with the serving woman? That was nothing. You haven't seen her temper yet, Arthur."

In the Heart of the Old Growth

ARTHUR'S PARTY ONLY MADE it a mile when her complaining began in earnest.

He was half-tempted to turn around and dump her back at the gates, even giving up the standard if he had to. But as he watched it bouncing in Drystan's capable hands, the banner hanging from the crossbar and the golden eagle perched atop it, he was sure he was on the right path. And if he had to deal with a spoiled, temperamental lady he'd been forced to marry, it was a small sacrifice he'd willingly make to save his people from the Saxons. Even if she was actively trying to destroy all of his marriages.

"You're going too fast!" she cried out, bouncing as she trotted on her horse.

"We have to move quickly while we have the roads. We'll slow down when we reach the forest and the marshes."

"I cannot go that fast, husband." She spat that last one, then growled and yanked on her horse's reins. Caius threw his head, mouth likely hurting from her abuse.

"Stop here, everyone," Arthur ordered, trying to keep the weariness from his voice. He hadn't slept enough the night before, what with her complaining and controlling and criticizing while they consummated their marriage. It had been an ugly business despite her beauty.

"Are you going back to retrieve my carrus now?" She sounded quite pleased with herself, having skipped straight over hope and jumped straight to expectation.

"No, I am not, Gwynafar." He said each word firmly as he patted his horse's neck. "You! Stay right where you are. And if you further abuse that horse's mouth..." He made a wrapping motion with his hands. "Bound. Gagged. Horse's ass."

She rolled her eyes and threw herself over Caius's mane with dramatic flair. "Don't you have any nice brothers you could marry me to?"

"Really? You think I'd beset them with you? Nay, lady. I'm not sure I'd wish you even on the Saxons."

Drystan stopped his horse beside Arthur's. "I don't know, Arturius. You seem to have a mighty weapon in this one. Unleash her on the battlefield, and she'll have them swimming back across the sea in a single day."

Gwynafar opened one eye and glared daggers at Drystan.

Arthur nodded his head up the road and began walking his horse. Drystan followed, and when they were out of her earshot, they stopped.

"Are you going to get the lady's carrus after all?"

Arthur snorted. "By the gods, I refuse! No. She'll need to ride with someone more experienced."

"Well," Drystan shrugged, "she's your wife. Why can't she ride with you?"

"I have a very strong feeling that she'll refuse. And if she doesn't, it's because she'll try to kill me."

Drystan's eyes widened, and he shook his head. "What do we do then? Set her loose?"

"We can't." Arthur pinched the bridge of his nose. "Strangely enough, her brother refuses to keep her. She's clearly not capable of surviving outside those walls. Within them, she needs her entire retinue, and even then, she's still not happy."

"Can't keep her, can't kill her."

"Aye. I'd like her to ride with someone else. I'm the only one she wants to kill. Oh, and Talara. And maybe you, now, too. I think that's all. At least for now."

"Here comes Lanslot."

"Arthur!"

"Not Lanslot," Arthur said softly to Drystan before the other man could hear him.

"Why?" Drystan asked, but it was too late for Arthur to answer. He wished he'd spoken earlier to Drystan of the way Gwynafar had been staring at Lanslot, how it made his ears burn to see her so boldly longing for his best friend.

He couldn't tell Lanslot, because the man only ever wanted to see the good in others, especially when it came to women. Even more so with ladies of a higher class. To his mind, they were inherently more honest, fragile, and good than the rest and in exceptional need of his protection.

"Arthur," Lanslot repeated, frowning. "What have you done? Why is your beautiful wife crying?"

"Talara? She doesn't cry."

Lanslot's frown deepened, and he shook his head sadly. "You know I meant Gwynafar."

"Then you shouldn't have called her beautiful as a distinction from my other wives," Arthur snapped. A headache was building in his right temple, so he massaged it with his fingers. "Were you going to suggest that she's more beautiful than—"

"No!" Lanslot waved his hands, backing away fiercely from the hole he'd started digging for himself. "But why is she crying?"

"She needs to ride with someone experienced who can keep her on the horse while we travel at speed."

"Why doesn't she ride with you?"

Arthur and Drystan exchanged a look.

"Because she's angry with him," Drystan answered for Arthur. "Do you think you could handle her?"

Lanslot's head jerked back, and a blush crept up his neck and into his cheeks. "I, uh, suppose. I mean, of course. I'm capable. Is that your wish, Arthur?"

Arthur didn't want to say yes. He wanted to roar "NO!" and every instinct compelled him to do so. But the headache now stabbing behind his right eye blunted his will. They didn't have time for this, and if he could trust anyone to do the right thing, it would be Lanslot. His honor would never allow him to be led terribly astray, even by the conniving snake of a woman that his new wife seemed to be.

"Please," Arthur finally said, and he stretched his neck. "We're already losing the day. We must travel as swiftly as possible."

"Of course, Arthur." Lanslot rode close to give him a pat on the back. "Everything will work out, and your new wife will warm to you, you'll see. She's simply scared, and she's lashing out to hide her fear. I'll sing your praises at every turn, old friend."

"I have no doubt." Arthur turned his horse, and the three friends cantered back to the main group.

Talara shot him a glance, tipped her head toward Gwynafar, and made a slashing motion across her neck.

Arthur shook his head firmly, then gave her a wink. He dismounted his horse and linked his hands together to help Lanslot onto Caius's back behind Gwynafar.

"May I take the reins, lady?" he asked her gently.

A burning pit grew in Arthur's stomach, but he pushed it down and jumped back onto his horse.

"Of course, sir. Thank you," she said, her light voice overly meek and submissive. It was anything but her true nature.

Lanslot reached forward, his arms stretching around Gwynafar's waist to take the reins and keep her balanced on the horse.

The distress she'd been wearing like a mask melted away into satisfaction, and she turned to Arthur. "I'm surprised you didn't ride with me, husband."

"I knew I'd only make you cry the whole way." He shrugged and turned his horse westward. Putting Gwynafar out of his mind as much as he could for the day, he focused his attention on their journey.

Thanks to the fair condition of the Via Augusta, they spent most of their day on the road and crossed a great distance in good time, despite their delayed start. Just north of Lindinis, they strayed from the road when it curved south toward Durnovaria, choosing a rutted dirt track leading west into the forest. The horses Aquila had given them were well-conditioned and brave, and, to Arthur's relief, none shied at the forest trail.

The forest was fresh growth at the edges where the surrounding towns and villages had steadily chopped away at it for centuries. But the deeper they traveled, the larger the trees became, their trunks thickening and the space between the trees growing. Bare branches sprawled like lightning against the gray skies, twisted and knotty as the trees emerged from the gauntlet of winter.

The warband kept a westerly route, occasionally turning north or south, but not for long, following the glowing globe of the early spring sun as it sank toward the horizon. When their path thinned to little more than a game trail, they found themselves in the heart of the old growth, surrounded by towering behemoths of oak, ash, and elm. Great pits and mounds from fallen trees marred the earth, leaving gaping holes like open wounds in the soil.

When the shadows grew long and dusk threatened to settle over the forest, Arthur called for his party to stop and set up camp. Talara helped him put up their tent while Gwynafar sat on a fallen tree, waiting for someone to start a fire. The small, easily portable tents set up in a circle around the fire were made with wool and leather and covered their many-layered bedrolls of furs and wool blankets.

Drystan had killed a boar while searching for firewood, so when he returned, he helped one woman, Aelwen, clean and cook it. By the time everyone had finished setting up camp and built a roaring fire with a good stockpile of wood to last the night, Aelwen and Drystan had roasted the boar and prepared a broth from pieces of boar fat and the wild garlic and thyme they'd foraged. Together they served the warband, and for the first time, Arthur noticed something between them.

A passing glance here. A lingering look there. The brush of one's hand against the other's. She was a humble beauty, but a strong woman and an expert archer like Talara. Brave, kind, and unforgiving in battle, she was one of the few women—along with his wives—that he trusted to be among his closest companions. But a romance with Drystan? He usually fell for women he couldn't have, the forbidden treasures. This would be the first healthy romance Arthur had seen spark his friend's genuine interest.

Arthur looked away, not wanting either of them to see that he'd noticed them. He also didn't want the others to see it if they hadn't already. He caught Talara's eye and motioned for her to sit beside him on a log near the fire. She hesitated at first but quickly relented, and he sat close to her, their shoulders touching, sharing a little body warmth in the cooling air.

"Still angry with me?" he asked, keeping his voice low as Drystan offered bowls of roast and broth to Arthur and Talara.

She sipped her broth and hummed, delighted, before answering. "Maybe a little. Just enough to keep it interesting, I suppose."

He grinned at that, and they enjoyed their dinner together in silence for a few moments.

"Where is your shiny new bride?" Talara asked, but she wasn't smirking. She was looking around the camp and the circle of tents with a frown.

Arthur took a giant gulp of his soup and a mouthful of roast boar before rising to his feet with his wooden bowl in hand. He stepped over the log and peered into his tent first, since it was where he and his wives would spend the night, but she wasn't there. After looking in all the other tents, that burning sensation hit the pit of his stomach again as he took a headcount. Eleven, including himself. Two heads were missing.

He took another massive bite of boar before setting his bowl next to Talara. "It seems she's wandered off."

And she wasn't alone.

A Strange and Haunting Melody

ARTHUR WALKED QUIETLY AS he searched the surrounding forest for his wayward bride, carefully placing each step so as not to make enough noise to forewarn the quarry of his approach. It took several long minutes of lingering between the quiet of the forest drenched in night and his lively companions relaxing around the fire after a hard day's ride. But then he heard them.

Two voices murmuring in the darkness, one troubled, the other plaintively.

He made his way closer and stuck to the trees, moving easily between them, mindful that the light of the fire would silhouette him. His heart beat faster in his chest as he got close enough to almost make out the words.

"He doesn't..."

"You don't understand..."

Arthur's chest tightened against his thudding heart, and his face burned with anger. It wasn't rational; he knew in his head. But in his heart, he could feel it. His best friend and his wife. Or the newest of his wives digging her talons into his best friend.

Anger dulled his awareness, and he stepped on a twig that snapped under his weight.

"Who's there?" Lanslot called out. The blade of his spatha rang lightly as he pulled it from the sheath.

Arthur rolled his shoulders, stood up straight, and walked out from behind the tree to face them.

Lanslot shielded his eyes with one hand, then resheathed his sword. "Arthur! What are you doing out here?"

"My wife was missing from camp. I didn't want her wandering alone in the dark."

"I'm not alone," Gwynafar said coolly.

"I can see that."

"I was merely sharing advice with your lady about—"

"Let's return to camp."

Lanslot put on a brave smile as he passed Arthur.

"Wife," Arthur grumbled, holding out his hand.

She slapped it away and walked past him behind Lanslot, but he snatched her by the arm and held her fast.

"Let me go," she hissed the words at him.

"Wait," he grumbled.

Lanslot glanced back, but didn't stop until he'd reached the camp.

"What are you doing out here?" He let her arm go, but leaned in so he could keep his voice low.

"I got lost," she answered with little enthusiasm.

"Whatever you think you're doing, you need to stop. There is too much at stake for me and my warriors to waste time playing your silly games."

"I'm not playing any games." She glowered up at him, her face barely visible in the faint light cast from the camp.

"I'm serious, Gwyanafar. You could have argued with your brother. You didn't have to agree to marry me and—"

"Yes," she snapped. "I did. Much like you, I did not have a choice."

Arthur remained silent as he considered that.

She crossed her arms over her chest. "I had hoped that you would be the same sweet boy I'd played with all those years ago, but you're not."

"It's time to grow up, Gwynafar. I've killed men, and almost lost my life more times than I can count."

"Couldn't you have at least pretended to be happy when you saw me? When my brother encouraged our marriage?"

A pang of guilt surprised him as he considered his own reaction and the way he'd dismissed her that first evening.

"I am sorry if I appeared less than pleased by the prospect of marrying you." He couldn't believe he was apologizing, but here he was. "My quest is—"

"And what of my wishes and desires? Is it my fate to live and die by the side of a man who doesn't fall to his knees at the sight of my beauty? A man too obsessed with his quest to let himself fall in love with me?"

Arthur suppressed the urge to scoff at her. "You have some strong notions about marriage, but this is no fairytale, Gwynafar. This is the burden of noble families. Alliances are built around marriages, and they serve the safety of all the people we take under our protection. We must make the best of this."

"How could I possibly make the best of," she gestured wildly at him with one hand, "this?!"

"Do what everyone in this camp has done. Put the needs of the many above your own."

"That, Dux Bellorum, is the philosophy of the warrior, and even that is selfishness veiled in honor. You don't fight for the people. You fight for your own glory, your own desires, and so people can worship you. No one is altruistic. Even if you feed the beggar and save a child from a burning home, you still do it because it makes *you* feel good and feeds your ego."

Arthur couldn't have imagined such a sheltered, self-centered woman would be so cynical and disillusioned, but he also knew it wasn't his job to change her mind.

"I saw the way you and Talara worked together, the quiet joy you share in each other's presence, and it made me sad. I can't believe we'll ever feel that way. So I wandered out into the forest for solitude, half-hoping some wolves might tear my body apart and end my misery." She choked back a sob, teary eyes glittering with reflected firelight. "Lanslot found me, and he tried to reassure me that you were a man I could come to love, just as everyone else does. He showed me kindness and compassion, and you chased him away because you're jealous and possessive."

Heat burned in his chest at the accusation, each word planting itself like a dagger in his heart. "Return to camp. Eat. You will share my tent. Do you understand?"

Gwynafar chewed her bottom lip, then turned and strode back toward camp.

Left feeling stunned, he found himself almost numb after bearing the weight of her words. Was he truly being a monster to a lady? To a woman who had bound herself to him through marriage?

He turned his head away from camp and stared into the darkness for several minutes until his vision adjusted. Sure that no one was following him, he walked deeper into the forest, too fast to be perfectly quiet. He needed distance, space, time to think with no one else's voice in his head.

Arthur didn't know how far he'd walked or for how long, but he found himself deep in the old growth surrounded by giant oak and yew. He touched a hand to each of them, offering his reverence and whispered respects to the spirits of the forest, then stood in the wide space between the trees so he could stare up into the night sky. The moon hung nearly full in the velvet sky, surrounded by glittering stars, and something about it called to him, tugging at his heart.

Something crunched in the dry old leaf litter behind him, and he spun to face it. The light of the moon illuminated the black canine's massive head and gleaming red eyes. Its head was held low and ears turned back, legs slightly bent, shoulders quivering with tension. The beast didn't growl a warning, but Arthur knew death when he saw it staring at him.

He reached for his spatha, but he fumbled uselessly where his scabbard should have been. The blade was back at camp, in his tent. His blood ran cold as he waited for the beast to make a move. He'd need to get it by the throat to stand a chance at surviving.

Arthur flexed his fingers, breathing shallow though his heart pounded and adrenaline pulsed through his veins.

The beast straightened its legs and picked up its head, ears relaxing, then walked slowly to Arthur. He had a sense the beast was a male, though he couldn't be sure right then. The creature's head reached as high as Arthur's hips, twice as large as any wolf he'd ever seen. The red slits of his eerie eyes softened, and he nudged one of Arthur's loose hands with a cold nose before turning and taking a few steps. He glanced over his shoulder expectantly, as if waiting for Arthur to follow.

The black dog's direction would lead Arthur deeper into the forest and farther away from camp, but something in the red glow of its eyes reminded Arthur of the war god's horse from his vision when he'd touched the King Stone, so he followed despite his better judgment. All was quiet in the forest, though he knew the creatures of the night were all around, slinking about, hunting their next meal, or even watching him as he passed through their domain.

The clinging cold of winter nipped at his skin, its frigid breeze burrowing into his neck, but he suppressed a shudder. He would enjoy the warmth of the fire when he returned from his walk with a messenger of the gods. His mind focused on the world around him, every small sound and every sensation, observing the ancient trees arching into the sky above him. Black skeletons against the blue of the moon-brightened midnight sky. In their own way, they sang the song of night, branches groaning in the breeze, the crisp, dead leaves at the bases of their trunks danced and chattered, and the scratch of their smallest residents scrambling up and down their bark.

They came out of the trees onto the grassy bank of a winding river, the wolf stopping at the very edge of the water and lying on his belly. He rested his head on his paws, but his red eyes rolled upward to watch the moon drift slowly through the sky above them. Arthur knelt beside the creature and reached forward, dipping his fingers in the icy water. He traced them back and forth, then splashed his face. The heat and ache of his pounding head dissipated with every splash, and the worries he'd carried to the water seemed to wash away downstream.

As the breeze picked up, it seemed as though the wind was singing, a feminine sound, as if a woman's beautiful voice echoed across the water, haunting in its strange, melancholy melody. Then he recognized words, ones that sounded to him like the words of Anieras and Talara when they chanted for rituals or led prayers. He listened for several heartbeats before he was sure the words in the woman's song were in the Druidic language.

That voice now singing to him was not merely the wind moaning and whistling through the bare tree branches.

And then he saw it, his body becoming still as he spotted the moon reflected on the inky surface of the gently flowing river, just as he had seen when he stared into the flames in the basilica at Calleva. Arthur had wanted so badly to take his visions as a sign that he was making the right decision to go next to Ynys Wintri, but he never considered that the things he saw in the flames might have been actual visions of what awaited him on his quest.

Just as in his vision, slender fingers broke the surface from below, breaking the waving reflection of the moon. Arthur dragged his hand from the water and watched, transfixed, as those fingers curled and the hand beckoned to him.

You Can't Save Everyone

Something within Arthur ached to go to her, urging him to dive into the frigid, black waters so he could hold that strange hand, but he gritted his teeth and resisted. He reached out a shaking hand and set it on the black wolf's back, hoping the sensation would ground his mind and body to reality.

The beast lifted his giant head and looked at Arthur, ears perked up, but he didn't growl or snap at the intrusion. He cocked his head, the tip of one ear flopping slightly, but his red-eyed gaze snapped back to the water, and Arthur followed it.

Now standing hip-deep in the water was a naked woman. Her wet hair lay around her breasts, water dripping down her soft stomach. Striking yellow eyes glowed so fiercely from her face that he couldn't discern her features. She continued her song as she waded toward him, her body moving like the surrounding water. Silhouetted by the moon, her hazy shadow stretched toward him across the lapping waves and onto the bank, reaching out with one ghostly hand before she did.

Arthur's breath caught in his throat, and the wolf barked sharply at the woman in the water. She stopped, turned her yellow gaze on the wolf, and the snaking shadow melted back into the rest of her shadow.

"Arturius," she said, her magical voice tickling his ear and washing his worries away. "Pendragon."

He nodded, unable to speak as the lilt in her voice lingered, caressing his mind with a gentleness that reminded him of falling in love with Talara. Softness, vulnerability, adoration.

"Yes," he answered, though his eyelids felt heavy, and he longed to lie in the brown, withered grass and sleep. "But I'm at a disadvantage, lady. I do not know you."

The glow of her eyes softened, and her mouth curved into a warm smile. "You know me, Arthur."

She stepped onto the bank, her nakedness displayed before him in shadow, and he averted his eyes to the grass at her feet.

"Look at me." The command was gentle, but it was a command nonetheless, and he obeyed.

Her skin shimmered, reflecting the moonlight on what appeared to be iridescent scales, and her form changed. The sharp angles of her face softened, her eyes shifted from yellow to deep brown, and the scales on her body rippled in tiny waves, transforming into cloth. When the rippling stopped, she was draped in flowing white robes.

"Do you remember now?"

Arthur's eyes stung as he gazed upon his aunt. At least, he'd been raised to believe she was his mother's sister. "Viviane?"

She held out her hand to him, but Arthur did not take it, and her loving smile faltered ever so slightly.

He had loved his aunt, and it had broken his heart when he'd found his mother in tears. She had told him that his Aunt Viviane would not return to Tintagel. All those years ago, he had grieved for her, believing she had died. Was this really her after all these years? Could he trust his eyes and ears?

Welcome the Siren, he heard the ghost king's voice whisper through his memory. He reached out and put his hand in hers.

"There's a good lad," she said, sounding just as she had the last time he saw her. Those slender fingers were warm but much smaller and more delicate than he remembered. But he supposed that it was he who had changed over the years lost between them.

"Forgive me, Lady Viviane, but how can I know it is truly you after all these years? I thought you had..." He tried to swallow the lump forming in his throat. That old grief roared to the surface, and remembering it was like tearing into an old wound that had already scarred over. The pain was greater than he could have imagined, aching in his chest and pounding in his head.

Viviane raised her free hand and smoothed back the unkempt locks from his forehead, then gently traced her fingers over the scar they'd been hiding there. "You were seven when you fell from your horse on our pilgrimage to Eryri. We were nearing the top when your horse stumbled, and you fell. We brought you into the sacred grove where your blood dripped from the wound to join the earth, and the gods allowed me to heal you."

"I remember," he said as images and sounds flashed through his mind. It was an incident he knew happened because his parents had never failed to bring up the time he'd almost died whenever they wished him to be more cautious and reserved in action. His own memories had been locked away, but now they flooded through him. The pain, the blurry vision, his father's worried voice, his mother's shrieks. The smell of his own blood.

"The gods chose me to heal you," Viviane said, her hand sliding gently from his face. She planted it over his heart, and the memories faded once more. "I have watched over you all of your life, even when you thought I was gone. The time has come for you to rise to your destiny, to claim your power."

"I am ready." Arthur said the words without thinking, but he did not regret them. Saving his people had been his sole focus since the first Saxon attack he'd witnessed, the one that had almost taken his father from this world to Annwn.

"Cynhyrfedd," she nodded toward the wolf, "tells me the gods have sent you. Do you understand why you are here now?"

"No." He sighed, body trembling with the rapid change of emotions that washed through him. "I've come to..."

What had he come to do? How did one welcome a siren?

"To welcome the siren," she said smoothly, then held her arms open.

Without a moment's hesitation, Arthur embraced the woman he'd known as his Aunt Viviane, and all the worry, fear, and self-doubt were washed from him. Her hug was as warm as it had always been when he was a child, the comfort instant and all-encompassing.

They pulled apart, and she cupped his face with one of her slender hands. "You have welcomed me, Arthur. It was easy, wasn't it?"

He chuckled. "A little too easy."

She nodded. "You are correct. There is more to this part of your quest than it would seem. When you befriended the eagle, you gained an ally. When you welcome me, you will gain knowledge."

"But..." He held up his palms. "I have welcomed you, aunt."

Viviane waggled a finger. Somehow, she managed to do even that gracefully.

"You must let go, Arthur. You must surrender to me."

He didn't like that word.

"I can't surrender. There is work to be done, lives to save. And we need to hurry before the Saxons have—"

She pressed a finger to his lips, silencing his words and stilling his anxious thoughts. Cynhyrfedd groaned loudly and rested his head on his paws again before closing his red eyes.

"You've already been so long at war and in leadership that you constantly fight for control of everything. But nature, life, the will of others, all these things are beyond your control." She removed her finger from his lips and gestured to the water. "You must surrender to fate, to destiny, and learn to move like the river."

"I don't understand," Arthur grumbled, staring out over the water. "Tell me what to do, aunt, and I will do it."

She arched an eyebrow. "You are not ready, but this is the song we must dance to if you are to succeed in your quest. Give me your sword."

Arthur opened his mouth to explain that it was back at his camp, but footsteps through the forest caught his ear, and he turned toward it. Even Cynhyrfedd twisted his head around to look.

Two figures stepped out of the forest and into the moonlight. Arthur's heart jumped into his throat when he recognized Talara. She carried his sheathed sword and offered it to him from her upturned palms. Beside her stood Myrddin, cloaked in dark brown robes and carrying the staff of Anieras. The eagle feathers hung from a leather thong tied near the quartz topping the staff.

"Myrddin?" Arthur breathed the name, unable to believe that the man could have found them so quickly.

The bard nodded his head almost imperceptibly, but he said nothing.

Viviane stepped forward and placed a hand on each of their shoulders. "You needed truth in love and friendship, and so I sent them to aid you. They join us now for the same purpose. Take your sword from your beloved."

Arthur reached forward slowly and grasped the spatha by its scabbard. He held Talara's quiet gaze, worried what she'd think of the midnight rendezvous with the mystical woman, but her eyes held no questions. That only made him worry more.

"Surrender your spatha, Arturius," Viviane instructed once more, holding out an open palm.

He placed the sword gently in her hand, bolting forward a step when she tossed it into the river behind her. But he was too late. It hit the surface with a splash and sank instantly.

Arthur curled his fingers in his hair, his blood hot as he stared at the quiet, flowing river. "What have you done?"

"Let go, Arturius. Your sense of control is an illusion."

He clenched his fists at his sides, and he saw red as he turned toward his favorite aunt. "That was my father's sword!"

"This will get harder if you do not surrender."

"I gave you the sword, passed down since before the Empire left this isle. What else could you possibly want?!"

She was unmoved by his distress, her dark eyes boring into him as she let the silence fill the space between them.

"It's gone," he said again, sick to his stomach that he'd lost the heirloom sword. It was as much a part of him as his own arm. Fighting with that sword was an urge that ran deep in his blood, a compulsion etched into his soul, and the loss of it opened a hole in his heart.

"Welcome me," Viviane reminded him.

Arthur clenched his jaw, biting back on the angry words he wanted to scream. He said through gritted teeth, "I already have."

"Surrender your friend, Arturius." She motioned Myrddin forward.

"No!" Arthur stared at her, horrified and unbelieving. "The river is freezing! It will kill him."

"Everything comes at a price, Dux Bellorum. Allies. Knowledge. Power. Saving your people and our way of life."

"I will not surrender Myrddin!"

"Then you will fail!" Her words thundered in his ears and echoed around him. "You lack resolve, Arthur. You lack courage. Greater than all these things, you lack faith."

"Myrddin," he muttered, staring into his friend's eyes. Arthur hadn't been as close to the bard as he was to his childhood friends, Lanslot and Drystan, but he was a friend. And he was one that Arthur had always felt responsible for protecting.

The bard stared back at Arthur, but he said nothing, and his face betrayed no emotion.

Arthur was torn between his desire to save his friend and the sacred quest with which the gods had entrusted him.

"Is this your wish? To die without a cause? Without a fight?" Arthur asked him.

"You are not in control, Arturius."

When she used his formal name, a pit of dread formed in his stomach.

Myrddin reached out to Viviane, and she took his hand. They walked to the edge of the river, and in the blink of an eye, she pushed him in. Two splashes followed as Myrddin and his staff plunged into the freezing black water. Arthur sank to his knees at the edge of the water and watched in numb horror as any trace of Myrddin disappeared into the flowing water.

He'd just gotten the bard back, and now he was gone for good, lost to the wicked demands of someone he thought he loved and trusted.

"This can't be happening," Arthur murmured as he watched the water for any sign of Myrddin, hoping that the man's instinct for self-preservation would send him bobbing to the surface so he could be saved, but he never emerged.

Arthur ached and fumed. The creature that had condemned the young bard to death could not be his kind, gentle, loving aunt from all those years ago.

"Who are you?" he growled as he pushed himself to his feet and faced her.

Her face remained neutral, though a touch of sadness now softened her dark eyes. "Your people will die, their blood spilled in violence as the Saxons raze the land and take everything you love." She nodded toward his wife. "Unless you have the strength needed to fulfill your quest."

"Welcome the siren," Talara said, her voice gentle as she stepped between Arthur and Viviane. "You are the great war chief. Your sacrifice will be great, but so will your victories."

She touched her warm fingers to his cheek, and her touch muted his fury.

He caught her hand and kissed her palm. "I want to save us all."

"But you can't save everyone, Arthur." Her hand slipped from his, and she walked to the edge of the water.

"Stop!" he cried. He grabbed for her, but she leaned just out of reach.

"If you can't save our people, what makes you believe you can save me?" With that, she stepped off the bank, splashing into the water and sinking instantly.

"No! Talara!" Arthur screamed her name. His heart breaking, he dropped to the ground, shot his arm into the freezing water, and grasped for her, but she was already swept away by the rushing river.

Sacrifices Have to Be Made

ARTHUR DIDN'T KNOW HOW long he'd remained on the ground, his forehead pressed to the cold earth, tears icy on his face as he mourned his beloved wife. He had no will to lift himself, no will to go on without her. The wolf whined and barked, and the sharp sound was just enough to spur Arthur to turn his head and open his eyes.

"On your feet, Arthur." The bottom of Viviane's robes filled his vision. "Do not bring shame to your ancestors."

He scoffed. "Is it shameful for a man to love his wife? How little should I have loved her? How does one know when he has loved too deeply?"

"There is no shame in love. It is the greatest necessity and luxury of life. But if you truly love them, you must do anything to protect them. Even if it means losing them."

"That is a contradiction."

She knelt and placed a warm hand on his back. "You must protect their hopes, their dreams, and their families, even if they go to Annwn before you." Standing again, she walked away. "Are you ready to do what must be done? Or is this where your journey ends, Arturius?"

His formal name was never far from her scolding tone. He didn't answer right away, instead staring numbly into the wolf's red eyes. All he could really see was Talara's sad face before she'd dropped into the water. Her gray eyes giving him a final, sorrowful look. The way her lips pursed when she was angry with him or transformed into a playful smile when she teased him.

"Is this the husband that gave Talara so much pride?"

"No." He hadn't wanted to answer, but the truth could no longer be caged. If Talara had seen him like this, she would have assumed he'd been struck with some illness or curse, and she'd call in every healer, shaman, and sorcerer from here to Caledonia.

He didn't want to go on without her, but he wanted her to be proud of him, whether they were reunited in Annwn or in the next life.

Arthur pushed himself from the ground into a kneeling position, then wiped his face and looked upward. The moon had almost finished her journey across the night sky, and the eastern reaches of darkness were already being chased by light. He stood, body aching from the cold, and faced Viviane. "What else do you require of me?"

Viviane did not smile. She did not seem pleased by his readiness to continue. "Welcome me, Arturius, by surrendering to destiny, to nature, to the great spiral of life, death, and rebirth."

"I am ready," he said, defeated and nearly bereft of any will as he thought about what she'd done earlier. He stood and faced her. "I surrender the illusion of control, and I offer myself."

She nodded curtly, then gestured to the river with one hand. "Everything you need to know to save the land from ravage and ruin will be revealed to you in the water, great dragon."

At one point, Arthur had thought that she might be some trickster sent to derail his quest, but that train of thought was only an excuse to deny the truth. The truth, he understood now, was that there were no simple answers, no secret weapons, no easy magic that would deliver him victory. There were answers, weapons, and magic in the world, but nothing would come quickly and without hardship. Every battle won would take something from him. Possessions, vitality, and, to his greatest pain, the people he loved most.

Arthur stepped off the bank and plunged into the frigid waters. The shocking cold pressed the air from his lungs, and when he was fully submerged, the current swept him away. He fought to hold his breath, but he didn't fight the current, letting it take him where it may. As the river tossed and turned him, he expected to scrape his limbs along the bottom or have his head smashed in by a rock, but he was carried along without harm done to him.

His stomach lurched as he came to a sudden stop, then he kicked his legs and pushed toward the surface as his lungs burned for air.

"Arthur!"

A blast of wind hit him, and he opened his eyes as he gasped for air.

As Arthur's muted senses sharpened again, he looked out on a great valley with a river running through it. He recoiled, crying out as heat seared against his face. Lifting his hands, he stumbled backward, smoke filling his nostrils. Coughing, he turned slowly, dizziness threatening to topple him, and found himself downwind of a great ritual fire. It roared in the pre-dawn air, its flames licking at the purple-gray sky. A series of wooden columns encircled the fire, and standing stones were set in a second ring just beyond. Most showed wear and weathering, but many appeared newer, likely replaced by the druids as they fell into disrepair. Beyond them was a clearing ringed by thick forest that sank with the slope down to the marshes. The top of the hill had been cleared so the land beyond could be viewed to the horizon.

Someone grabbed him by the arm and dragged him away from the fire. He let the strong hand pull him around the fire, his eyes stinging and blurry from the smoke, but he quickly breathed clean air. A half-hearted cheer rose as Arthur rubbed his eyes, and when his vision cleared, he found his warband huddled in front of him. The standard with the golden eagle bobbed as the bearer held it aloft to welcome him.

The person who'd taken him away from where he'd been standing too close to the flame was Rigana. Her red curls hung loose about her shoulders, fluttering in the morning breeze, and her green eyes were filled with worry as she studied him.

"You aren't hurt?"

"No," he said, though he wasn't sure. There was a hole torn out of his heart, but he was sure that wasn't the wound she was referring to.

How could he tell her about her hearth-sister?

His mouth worked, but he couldn't form the words. "Rigana?"

"How did you get here so quickly?" She leaned close and lowered her voice. "Husband, I raced here to find everyone looking for you in a panic. You've been missing for at least a day. Myrddin told us to come here and light the sacred fire. Said that it would bring you. I didn't believe it, but..." She forced a smile as tears welled in her eyes. "I'm glad we listened."

Arthur didn't usually show affection to his wives in front of his warriors, but he was so relieved to see her and comforted to have her by his side again that he wrapped her in his arms. He wove his fingers into the soft curls of her wild hair and kissed her hard. She returned his passion without hesitation, restoring his spirit and warming a little of the ache in his heart.

His warriors surrounded them, huddling to clap his shoulders and cheer his return more heartily this time.

When he broke his embrace with Rigana, he turned to greet each of his warriors. Lanslot first, then Drystan and Aelwen. They all took turns clasping arms with him and expressing their relief at his appearance. Gwyanafar was last among the group to greet him, but he wouldn't allow himself to be bothered by it. She didn't like him, and she wasn't happy with him, so he imagined she wasn't thrilled that he was found alive. But she put on an air of propriety as she greeted him.

"I'm thankful for your safe return, husband." She paused, glancing toward Lanslot, then leaned up on her tiptoes and gave him a peck on the cheek. Her skin was paler than usual, and there were dark circles under her eyes. Surely she'd slept well without him in their tent, hadn't she?

"And I am glad to see you, wife," he lied, hoping it could be the start of a less hostile relationship between them.

He turned back to Rigana as her earlier words registered in his mind. "Myrddin told you to light the sacred fire?"

"Yes," a man answered. "I did."

The warriors parted to reveal a young man in dark brown robes carrying an intricately carved wooden staff topped with crystal quartz and eagle feathers.

"Myrddin?" Arthur whispered, taking a few tentative steps toward him.

The bard pinned his gaze to the earth at his feet and wrung his hands nervously around the staff. "I apologize, Dux Bellorum. I was grieving and—"

Arthur bolted forward and squeezed the younger man in a crushing hug. His eyes stung with the threat of tears, but he fought to keep them from falling. His people needed his strength, and none needed it more than this warband. He pulled back, clapping Myrddin's shoulders.

"I..." There were so many things he wished to say, but this wasn't the best time or place. They had roads to travel and a witch to find. "I'm overjoyed that you've returned to us. We'll need to talk when next we make camp and—"

The realization struck him like a bolt of lightning. If Myrddin was here...

"Where is Talara?" Arthur roared, spinning to study the faces of his warriors.

Before anyone could answer, footsteps could be heard coming up the hill. All turned to face the only pathway, and as soon as her proud head bounced into view, Arthur sprinted for her.

He met the confused woman and lifted her off her feet to embrace her. Passion, love, and gratitude overwhelmed him as he kissed her fiercely, not stopping until his lungs ached for air. She smelled of mint and horses. When he broke the kiss, he pressed his forehead to hers and ran one hand over her thick black hair.

"You're safe," he finally said, wishing he didn't have to pull away from her.

She cocked her head and looked him up and down. "I'm just fine. You're the one we were all worried about. Where have you been, love?"

"I welcomed the siren," he said simply, swallowing against the lump of fear, pain, and sadness still in his throat as he remembered clearly the sight of Talara plunging into the dark waters.

"That part of your quest is already done?" She sounded disappointed.

"I believe it is, but we must make our offerings to the gods and bring another offering to the water." He looked around once more, this time fully taking in the view of the glittering lakes and misty marshlands surrounding the great hill and the strong, wide River Brosca flowing to the south. "What is this place?"

"Ynis Wintri." She squeezed his hand, grinned, and took a deep breath. "Something about this place just feels... right."

"Is it your first time here?" He felt bad that he didn't know the answer. His parents had taken him to all the most sacred sites in the land, but he knew everyone had not had the opportunities he'd enjoyed.

"Yes. But I can see why it's named the Isle of Glass."

The orange and pink sky reflected on the water as dawn neared, and he wished they could spend the day in admiration of the beauty of this ancient sacred space. But it was not to be. The words had not been spoken aloud by any god or mortal, but his intuition warned him they were running out of time. "If you truly love it, I'll bring us back here. I swear it."

She nudged him playfully. "Are you sure you're all right?"

He tugged the edge of her cloak and brought her along as he returned to Myrddin. "Please, bard. Lead us now to make our offerings to the gods."

"It's already finished. At the end of my ritual, you appeared from the other side of the sacred fire."

Arthur wanted to linger, but knew they couldn't. He hoped a day when he could return and stay longer wasn't too far in the future.

"Talara? Do you have my spatha?"

"I didn't see it at camp, so I thought you had it."

He shook his head. Sacrifices would have to be made, he remembered all too well, and it was better for Viviane to keep his sword than for her to keep Myrddin or Talara. Wondering what he could add to the offerings, he walked while warriors murmured about his mysterious return.

Arthur wanted to thank the spirits and the gods for the hard wisdom gifted to him, and for allowing him to return to his people. "Walk with me? And bring Myrddin."

Together they walked the hillside, exploring the isle and watching the marshy world below wake with the rising of the sun. When they were out of earshot of the rest of the warband, Myrddin was first to speak.

"I was angry with you, Arthur. For days I wandered in search of the eagle, and I cursed your name. I begged the gods to strike you for abandoning me."

Arthur wanted to argue that he hadn't abandoned his young friend, but he couldn't. It was the ugly truth.

"But I heard him. I heard my grandfather speaking to me. He told me to surrender my anger and my pride, to put away my grief until our quest is won. So I went to Caer Cadwyr and found Rigana. She made me beg, but finally let me join her to return to you. I... I'm sorry I didn't follow you. I regret walking away from my sacred duties." He paused and faced Arthur. "Can you forgive me?"

"There is nothing to forgive between friends, Myrddin. You deserved more time than I gave you. I hope that, with time, you can forgive my haste. I respected and admired Anieras, and I have missed his wisdom and guidance."

Myrddin's eyes reddened, welling with tears, and he shook his head. "As you said, there is nothing to forgive between friends."

A pair of eagles whistled happily in the sky above, their wings buffeted by the wind as they soared, and Arthur smiled, imagining the joy and tales Anieras would have shared if he had been there to see them.

"Look," Talara said, stooping to pick up a willow twig. "I'll take it as a sign."

Myrddin snorted. "We're surrounded by marshes. The willow trees are everywhere."

"We can choose to accept signs, or we can choose to ignore them. You should know that better than I."

"May I have it as an offering?" Arthur asked, and she passed it to him, brushing his fingers with hers as she released the budding twig in his hand.

They walked toward the center of the hill and stood quietly together, each softly whispering their own prayers as Arthur made his offering to the gods. He tossed the twig into the blaze and watched the flames curl and eat it.

"I have news from Caer Cadwyr and our journey here," Myrddin said, also watching the willow twig burn.

"Good news, I hope."

The bard shook his head. "Refugees swarm to Caer Cadwyr. And they swear the Saxons have a dragon, and it's destroying everything in its path as it marches west."

The Great Mountain

Dragons were creatures of the most ancient legends, though most villages and towns had their local stories to scare children into good behavior. Arthur had always heard that the elusive creatures had stuck to the mountains, but he suspected that there was nothing left of the creatures but whispers anymore.

"Did they see this dragon?" Arthur asked, keeping his voice level.

"Aye. They saw it. A great white beast with skin like a snake and wings like a bat. They said it attacks from both air and ground. According to their reports, the beast even breathes fire. The dragon and its masters could be at Londinium in as little as three days, more if they're intent on clearing the countryside of everyone and everything that isn't them and their mercenaries."

"And that means Calleva could be next. If they keep going, they could burn the land all the way to Tintagel."

"Every moment we delay..."

"I know." Arthur flexed his fingers, and they ached to grip the hilt of his spatha again. "The offerings have been given. I'll offer one more, on your advice, to the waters here."

The offering would actually be for Viviane, but he wasn't ready to explain his meeting with her to anyone else yet.

"I'll advise on the offering," Myrddin agreed somberly. "But I need to know your intentions."

"I wish to give thanks for wisdom, strength, and for the divine."

"Will you help me collect some things from the forest?" Myrddin asked Talara. "Your husband needs to ready the men."

"Wait." Arthur held up a hand as he turned in a circle. "Where are the horses?"

"Where we left them," Talara said. "We reached the isle by water. The locals lent us their boats."

"And you know our next destination?" Myrddin asked.

"I believe I do." Arthur turned back toward the sacred fire to gather his warriors and share what Myrddin had heard about the Saxons. "I'll share what it is after we've made the offering at the water's edge and returned to the horses."

Arthur accepted a yew garland woven with rosemary, sage, and mugwort, laid it on the water, and sent it bobbing across the surface of the lake. Rigana handed him a silver coin, a miliarense issued under Julian II. Arthur rubbed the face of the coin and inspected it one final time. It had been an early gift from his grandfather, and he'd held onto it for luck. Julian's face graced the front, and a fully armored soldier had been stamped on the back, a spear erect in one hand as he leaned against the shield at his legs.

"This coin represents the virtue and courage of the army," Arthur repeated the words his grandfather had told him. "The strength and honor that men must show in battle for the good of the people they defend."

He kissed the coin before gently tossing it into the water just beyond the floating wreath of yew and spring herbs.

"On with our quest," Arthur called to his warband. They cheered in response, shaking spears, bows, and shields before climbing carefully into the borrowed cwrwgl coed, each boat carved from a single tree. The soft wood vessels could fit three warriors each, so the band was split up into five smaller groups.

Arthur took the lead with Talara and Myrddin, too stricken by Viviane's hard lesson to let his friend and wife be too far away from him, and they pushed out into the water. Talara sat in the front to direct their passage, while Arthur and Myrddin paddled. In another boat, Drystan and Aelwen were joined by a spearman.

Gwynafar perched at the front of a boat, glowing like the moon in her impractical white dress, blonde hair hanging loose down her back. Behind her sat Lanslot, as to be expected these days, and one of the spearmen with whom he was close. Arthur gritted his teeth and turned his head away.

Arthur didn't trust Gwynafar. He should have trusted Lanslot, his friend since boyhood, but the ride on horseback from Calleva had put an unspoken distance between the two men. Since then, Lanslot and Gwynafar had never been found far from one another.

He brushed his paranoia away, knowing greater worries lay ahead. As his boat approached the offering wreath floating on the quiet water, Arthur brought his fingers to his lips and touched them to the wreath. His boat stopped suddenly, jerking so harshly that Talara nearly tumbled out of the prow.

Shouts of alarm rang out, mingling with questions about whether they'd run aground already, but before Arthur could answer them, a familiar slender hand slipped from the water and grabbed him by the wrist, hurling him out of his boat and into the water. The chilly morning water shocked his system, and he opened his eyes to find Viviane's face in front of him, her wild black hair waving around her head in the gentle current.

Arthur wanted to move, to push himself to the surface, but her hand held him tight, and she transfixed him with her gaze. He heard more splashes, though they were muted by the water. In his periphery, he could see clearly his friends swimming toward him, but the water grew murky with their splashing.

Viviane's hard face softened with that gentle, loving smile he'd seen so often as a child. She pressed the hilt of his missing sword into his free hand and closed his fingers around it.

"I blessed this sword for your forefather, a great Roman general. I loved him, and he loved me true, so I have spent the centuries watching over his progeny. This sword is named Excalibur. It will carve out your victory for another forty-three years, but when you pass to Annwn, it must be returned to me."

Arthur nodded, his head pounding and his lungs aching for breath.

"In three dawns, it will help you call the dragon. You must complete your quest before then, Arturius, or all you love will be lost." She pulled the sword from his hand to tie its scabbard to his belt. Then she reached to the side, roughly pulled a stunned Talara through the water, and pushed her against Arthur's chest. "She can't hold her breath as long as you can."

The bottom had been stirred too much by the splashing of his warband as they'd fallen in the water, and the murk now obscured

Viviane's face. Arthur's vision darkened, but when he tried to kick this time, his limbs obeyed.

He banged his head against something at the surface, opening his eyes to find a layer of ice at the top of the water. This could not be the marshlands he'd fallen into. There had been no ice on the water, and it hadn't been cold enough to snow for weeks. Clutching Talara's weakening body against him with one arm, he used the other to smash his fist against the obstruction.

Once, twice, three times. On the fourth strike, it cracked, splitting apart, and Arthur rocketed upward. He broke the surface of the water into the freezing air and sucked wild breaths into his burning lungs. Talara choked and sputtered against his chest, and he pulled her along as he pushed the cracked slabs of ice from his path. Freezing rain pelted him from above, sending a chilling ache through his bones. He had to stop and tread water several times so he could smash more ice, clearing a path for himself and for the rest of his warband as they bobbed to the surface and swam after him. This was a mountain top lake, nothing like the warmer marsh water where he had last seen Viviane.

When he finally crawled onto the shore and lay on the snow-covered earth, he and Talara both shook violently from the cold, teeth chattering and the urge to sleep almost too strong to fight.

"W-we have to s-start a f-f-fire," she ground out through her chattering teeth, though her head remained pressed to his chest.

Arthur silently agreed, unable to speak, and yanked his frozen clothing from hers before rising to his feet. He stood hunched, hugging himself against the cold, breath puffing white clouds in front of his face as he looked around. They'd emerged from an ice-covered lake surrounded by mountain ridges, and on the west side of the lake, a great, snow-topped mountain soared into the sky. It was exactly the mountain from the vision he'd seen in the ritual fire at Calleva.

He remembered then that he'd also seen a woman pointing at the mountain.

The witch.

Arthur spun in a circle, but the barren landscape showed no sign of life other than his warriors, who were on the verge of freezing to death. He spotted a formation of wooden posts in a circle on the nearest ridge and marched shivering toward it as his people splashed onto the shore behind him. He caught a quiet humming as he neared the structure and thought it must be the cold affecting his hearing, but the sound grew louder as he got closer to the posts.

The humming became a strong vibration when he grew near enough to the posts to recognize the ogham and legendary scenes intricately etched into the wood. The sensation disrupted his hearing, and his head felt numb as he fought through knee-deep snow for every step, but he kept going, his intuition insisting that the answers he sought lay in that ritual circle. A sizzling sound preceded a jagged arc of lightning between the posts, and a swirling wind blew the snow clear of the center.

Arthur jumped as an arc zapped and danced between the posts. Arc after arc connected the posts, ending in a blinding flash of white lightning. A blast of icy wind and a bolt of lightning shot out of the circle and threw him backward into the wet, frigid snow. He lay there a moment, stunned, as his clothes turned rigid and froze to his wet skin. His breathing slowed as he rested.

"Get up!" a woman shrieked at him, but she sounded so far away. He thought he heard the frightened whinny of horses, but he had to be imagining it. There was nothing in this place.

"I need to rest," he insisted, the words barely whispering past his numb lips. "Only for a moment."

He closed his eyes as the numbed sensation of many hands on his body brought more comfort than worry.

Whose hands? He wondered as his mind drifted to the beauty of the great mountain. The image swirled away like smoke in the wind as he dwelled on the question. He remembered his people, his warriors. His friends.

His wives.

Arthur shot himself back to consciousness and forced his eyelids open, groaning in pain as bits of flesh and eyelashes were torn away. "Rigana! Talara!"

He wanted to fight against the hands holding him, stand on his own two feet, and find the women who would love him through his best and worst days. For them, he would forgo his rest and wear his weariness like a crown.

"Hold still," a gentle voice said.

"Talara?"

"Quiet," Talara hushed him. "The witches have come."

A Winding Maze of Paths

WHEN ARTHUR OPENED HIS eyes again, his eyelids stung, but he was greeted by quiet and warmth. A fire crackled gently, and after sitting up and rubbing his eyes, he found himself lying in a roundhouse near a hearth around which the members of his warband slept under thick wool blankets. The room was cozy and warm from the fire, and though Arthur's body was sore, the heat had chased away the ache from his bones. Rigana and Talara were on either side of him, and he smiled in relief to see they had both survived the frozen lake. He took a quick headcount of the sleeping bodies and breathed his thanks to the Morrigan that none of his warriors had been taken.

Not yet.

He could have rested longer, but he remembered Viviane's words. Three dawns was all he had to finish his quest, and his eagerness made him restless.

Careful not to wake either of the women, Arthur slipped from between them and stood, taking his blanket with him to find a spot against the far wall where he could simply sit and stare at the fire. His throat was parched, and his stomach rumbled with hunger, but he didn't see any sign of food or drink, so he stayed put and kept quiet.

Time passed without mark as he considered how far they'd come and how far they had yet to go. There was less time left than he'd thought, but he knew the costs would be greater, as Viviane had warned.

And that was her gift to him, her lesson: the understanding that he needed the strength of spirit to keep fighting no matter how much he lost and the wisdom to understand that his reasons for fighting transcended the present. What he won in victory would outlast his own life and the lives of the people he loved. Knowing that all he loved would leave this world regardless of his victory had changed something within him. It had hardened his heart and steeled his resolve to win.

"Lost in thought?" Drystan asked as he sat down beside Arthur and passed him a waterskin and a chunk of hard bread.

"I was." Arthur gulped the water until he emptied the skin, then nibbled at the bread. "Why aren't you sleeping?"

"We were all worried about you. We thought..." He swallowed the words and lightly punched Arthur's leg. "Your sword is by the hearth."

"Thank you." Arthur finished the last bite of bread and wiped the crumbs from his fingers. "What have you seen?"

Drystan sighed and shook his head. "Great magics. That circle you were heading for? Did you... see what it did?"

"I saw the lightning and the snow, then nothing."

"Our horses and all our supplies were in that circle by the time we reached you."

"What?" A chill rolled down Arthur's spine as he waited for Drystan to finish the joke, but his friend only nodded.

"How did we fall into the water at Insula Avallonis and come up in a different lake? And the horses we hadn't seen in at least half a day appear out of thin air in one of the druids' circles?" He shook his head again and ran a hand through his short auburn hair. "I'd never believe it if I hadn't lived it. I still can't say whether this is all a dream."

"I can't say I know either."

"That doesn't make me feel better," Drystan grumbled, then chuckled wearily.

Arthur chewed the inside of his cheek for a moment before finally asking the question he'd thought better of asking since Drystan sat with him. "And what have you seen of Gwynafar?"

Drystan groaned and nodded somberly. "I don't trust her as far as I could throw her, and I could throw that one pretty far. If I was the kind of monster who would throw a lady. But that one is begging for it."

"And our childhood friend. Have you noticed anything?"

"His attachment to your third wife? Yes. He clings to her like a moth to a flame, and she is naught but flame."

"What do you suppose he's thinking?"

"That you're too rough a husband for a highborn lady, too battle-worn, too unfeeling. And I know that because he said as much when I suggested he might be spending too much time with her."

"Have you heard her speak to him?"

"Only in hushed tones. She's careful, sneaky. Her words to him are left between the two of them alone."

"You'd think we could all focus on the Saxons as enemies."

"Some people love enemies more than they love friends."

Arthur turned his face and locked eyes with Drystan. "Do you stand with me or with him?"

Drystan scoffed, then clutched a hand to his chest. "Oh, how you wound me, Arturius!"

But Arthur did not laugh. He did not blink.

"Of course I stand with you. I always have, and I always will. To stand with him would be to stand with that witch, and I don't mean witch in a good way, like those that brought us here."

"Those that brought us here?"

"Ah. Yes. You were struck by lightning, the horses appeared with all our supplies, and nine witches met us at the circle."

"That's a rather big detail to forget."

"I was just saving it for when you felt better. But I'm still worried about the other part. Do you really believe Lanslot would turn on you? He is smitten with Gwynafar, but he's loyal to a fault, Arthur. He would never betray you."

"You're probably right."

"You're tired, so your mind is working too hard. Don't jump at shadows, old friend. There's still a lot of work to be done."

"So, the witches."

"Yes. Lovely women, some young, some old. Led by a silver-haired beauty who calls herself Eilinor. They led us here and made sure we were warm, dry, and well-fed before they let us sleep."

"How long have we been here?"

Drystan shrugged. "I don't know when we arrived in this place, but we were here a few hours before everyone went to sleep."

"The witches found us by the mountain. It's like my vision. This should be the final piece to my quest." Arthur thudded his fist against the floor, eager for battle, hungry for victory.

"What about this dragon I've heard Myrddin and your first two wives discussing?"

"The Saxons have a dragon. And when I touched the King Stone—"

"Gods, what a fucking day that was." Drystan rubbed his temples. "I was sure you were dead that time. Come to think of it, you've been doing that a lot lately."

Arthur sighed and continued. "The king told me I must befriend the eagle. The eagle was King Aquila. And I'm learning more each day about what I've sacrificed in order to gain that man as an ally. Then he said I had to welcome the siren."

"Wait. The witches are sirens?"

Arthur shook his head. "No. I met the siren when I disappeared from camp."

"And what did she give you?"

"The Lady of the Lake granted me... Perspective. Wisdom. She helped harden my heart for what is to come."

"That doesn't sound like a gift." Drystan frowned.

Arthur shrugged. "She also blessed my sword and returned it to me."

"Well, magical blessings of swords and a hardened heart from a wet sorceress, that's a mighty boon."

Stifling a laugh, Arthur elbowed Drystan sharply in the side.

"Ow! Hey!"

"Quiet, or you'll wake the others," Arthur teased.

"So what's the last part, Dux Bellorum?" Drystan put a mocking emphasis on the title.

"I must champion the witch." Arthur shrugged. "I don't know what that means. Or what it'll cost."

"Well, you're in luck! We wandered into a village full of witches. It's a pretty town, ancient and walled. All the houses are round, like in the old stories."

"And how far are we from the lake?"

"Maybe an hour's walk, at least in knee-deep snow when you're wet and nearly freezing to death." Drystan turned his gaze to the fire and crossed his arms behind his head as he leaned back against the wall. "I'm bloody glad to be in here instead of out there. What's that?"

Arthur followed his gaze to one of the thatch-shuttered windows. "What do you see?"

Drystan rose and moved across the room, Arthur following. He placed his finger against the hardened mud and straw at the edge of the window, and a ray of pink light beamed across his skin.

"Sunlight."

Both men jumped as the door to the roundhouse opened, and a woman in black stepped inside. She closed the door behind her but stopped when she spotted Arthur and Drystan staring at her.

"Come with me," she whispered from beneath the hood of her heavy black cloak, gesturing for them to follow her.

Arthur stepped carefully between his sleeping warriors to grab Excalibur from near the hearth before following her. She pointed at a line of cloaks hanging along the wall, and both men donned one.

A blast of freezing, snow-filled air hit them in the face when they stepped outside, and Arthur remembered the fear he'd felt at nearly succumbing to the cold. He pulled his hood down over his face and wrapped his cloak more tightly around his body, then hurried after the woman in the black cloak. She led them through a winding maze of paths between the round buildings with thickly thatched roofs.

As much as he wanted to make a better mental map of the village, the blizzard made it hard to even keep sight of the woman rushing ahead of them. The woman stopped at the door to a hut larger than the rest he had seen, then ushered Arthur and Drystan inside. Leaving behind the blowing snow and frigid air, they found nine women seated at a long table raised above the rest of the room.

In the center of the table sat a woman taller than the others, draped in robes so white that even Gwynafar might have been impressed. She looked to be as old as Arthur's mother. Her lean, angular, proud face bore lines around her eyes and at the corners of her mouth, but she looked as regal as any queen and more beautiful still. White-silver hair hung straight around her face, shining in the firelight at the center of the room. The women seated to her left wore cloaks in varying shades of blue, and those to her right wore varying shades of green.

"Arturius," the lady in white said, rising from her seat and bowing her head ever so slightly. The other women followed her example, and after she took her seat, they resumed theirs. "I thank you for coming to my aid."

He wasn't sure what to say, considering he hadn't meant to come here through the lake, and he didn't even know where here was. "Yes, lady," he bowed his head in return. "I have come to be your champion."

"And who has said I need a champion?" She arched one dark gray eyebrow, and he noticed her bright green eyes.

"An ancient king tied to the land at the King Stone with his cursed warriors."

One corner of her mouth lifted into a half-smile, and her eyes softened. "Tegid." She turned her face to the woman next to her. "Still looking after me."

"He always will, Eilinor."

"As much as I'd love to toy with you, Tegid and Viviane have begged me not to, so let us speak swiftly and true. I know of your quest. And I believe I know what I need to give you. Though my beloved and my sister insist you are worthy, I haven't had the chance to be convinced yet."

"How may I prove myself, lady?"

She stood again and pushed her chair back, but this time, the other ladies remained seated.

"I know you are eager to go to battle," she said as she walked around the table and stepped down from the dais to come closer, looking at him as if evaluating a horse. "You are anxious to fight for our people, to fight as the chosen hero of the gods, but there are many things I must show you first."

"I worry I am running out of time," Arthur said, clasping his hands behind his back to keep from fidgeting with them. "The dragon will be called on the dawn of the third day—"

"I know. The dawn that rises now is your second day."

"Already?" Drystan asked, and he sounded as shocked as Arthur felt.

"Drystan. Would you join my ladies for breakfast while I speak with your war chief? They long to hear tales of your renowned bravery."

The big man turned red in the ears, his eyes wide in surprise. "Renowned? I have some tales, but they might bore such fine—"

"Nonsense." She waved a hand, dismissing his concerns. "Please. I will keep your leader safe."

He glanced at Arthur, who gave a subtle nod, then stepped onto the dais and accepted a seat that was offered on the opposite side of the table from the waiting ladies.

"Come," Eilinor said, linking arms with Arthur. "We haven't a moment to waste if we're going to call the dragon."

An Oath Broken

EILINOR LED HIM TO a door opposite from where Arthur had entered with Drystan. When they walked out, he braced for the blizzard but found a warm spring awaiting. The air was pleasantly cool, and the snow had vanished. Sunlight smiled down from a clear blue sky. Flowers waved at him from lush, green grass. They crested a small hill, and he could see the lake and the ritual circle on the ridge.

Arthur rubbed his eyes. "Is this real?"

"It is real."

"Where are we?"

"Not where. When. We are in my village, Din Gwiddon, but we are here at the end of the last spring. My favorite time of year is when the flowers are blooming and all the toil of spring blooms into the joy of sweet summer." She bent to pluck a flower with six large white petals. "The Eryri lily," she said, then passed it to him.

"Thank you, but—"

"Oh, and this one." She plucked a five-petaled violet flower and passed it. "One more," she mumbled, tapping a long finger to her chin. "Ah!"

Eilinor strode down the hill and stooped to pick another flower. "This."

Arthur accepted the yellow flower and studied its five broad petals. "These are... quite pretty, lady. But why do I need flowers? Are these an offering?"

She laughed loudly and took his arm again. "Of course they're an offering, Arturius. They're for your wives. Are men so war-bound in this new age that they forget to do lovely small things to make their wives smile? And you! You have *three* wives. Tell me you're the happiest you could possibly be."

Arthur avoided her gaze, looking instead at the flowers. "I am a fortunate man."

Her smile faded. "Choose one flower for each of your wives. When we return, they will join us for our morning meal, and you will present each of them with your chosen flower."

"I understand," he said curtly. While he wanted to see his wives smile, he knew they'd be mournful and gutted if the towns and people they loved were burned and eaten by some Saxon dragon.

"Ah. Yes. So much to tell you. I get distracted by love, Dux Bellorum, you must forgive me." She took a deep breath and led him through the village gates to look out over the lake far below. "The Saxons have brought more than mere men this time. Your people have battled bravely, but the Saxons have seen the weariness of war upon their foes, smelled the growing weakness of resolve, and they intend to do more than plunder and pillage. They wish to settle our beautiful isle with their own families."

"You mean invade."

"It is an invasion, but there is an opportunity, Arthur. Most of them want to bring their families here and farm, nurturing and harvesting the great bounties of the land. But the lines of Hengist and Horsa..." Her glittering green eyes darkened. "Those men brought their magic. They spoke the darkest words of magic, bathed in the blood of our people so thoroughly that their line will always thirst for the blood of the tribes of our land. From Tintagel to Dubris, and from the Ériu to Caledonia, they will murder, raze, and destroy everything in their path."

"How do we fight this magic?"

"We fight their gods with our gods, their magic with our magic, men with men, creatures with creatures."

"Those fleeing say the Saxons have a great white dragon, a beast that breathes fire. Why would the gods want me to call it? Am I to fight it myself, or with my warband?"

She turned her gaze toward the lake, her jaw tightening. "I cannot give you all the answers. I can give you merely what you need to fulfill your quest and claim victory, but know that there is a cost for every gift you're given. Wisdom, strength, power, magic."

"I..." He swallowed the pain rising in his throat again at the memory of losing Talara. Even though it hadn't happened, he couldn't shake the mental scar it had left. "I understand."

"Viviane tells me so, but I can't help but emphasize that truth to you. It's as critical as anything else I could give you."

"We know the stakes, lady. Tell me how I can be your champion."

"Let us return to the hall for dinner with your people."

Arthur stumbled to a stop. "You said we'd be back when they were ready to join us for breakfast!"

"Come now." She patted his arm and tugged him along. "If I'd told you we wouldn't be back until dinner, you wouldn't have come along for our little talk. I'm saving us both the time, and I'm saving you trouble. Besides, magic takes effort, and our little trip to the end of last spring served an important purpose! Now, be a good man and open the door for a lady."

He bit back his frustration and did as she asked, opening the door to the roundhouse and returning the same way they'd left. A shock of cold nipped at his neck as he entered, and he found the blizzard had resumed outside that door. Arthur's stomach rolled with nausea, but he said nothing as he followed the lady back into the hall.

His warband was seated at many wooden tables in the shape of perfect circles, feasting on roast meats and vegetables, broth, and a honey mead so rich he could smell it even above the food. Myrddin alone sat with the witches, singing them a melancholy tune over his mead.

Talara bolted from her seat to greet him. Rigana stood slowly, but she was just as eager to see him. Gwynafar had been smiling as she sat next to Lanslot, but she frowned when she spotted him.

"Gift the flowers to your wives, Arturius," Eilinor commanded, her voice rising above the noise of the hall without shouting or even sounding strained. "Lady Gwynafar? Join your hearth sisters in greeting your husband."

Myrddin's singing stopped, and all the conversation in the hall quieted as they watched the witch queen's ritual. Gwynafar dipped her head to their hostess before gracefully lifting herself from her seat. She walked to Arthur so smoothly she almost seemed to float, and she did a poor job of hiding her satisfaction at entrancing the entire hall with her movements.

"Rigana, first of my wives," Arthur addressed the fierce beauty before handing her the purple flower.

"You may show your wives affection, great war chief." Eilinor certainly seemed to enjoy his discomfort at having everyone watch this demonstration. But he had to prove himself, and if all he had to do was sacrifice his comfort by showing love to the women who held the pieces of his heart, then he would consider himself fortunate this time.

It was a small price to pay, and he would happily oblige the queen of the witches.

Arthur kissed Rigana, and she returned it with more passion than he'd expected. His warriors cheered, and his ears grew hot as he listened. She finally released him, grinning up at him before pushing him toward Talara to her left.

"Talara, second of my wives." He placed the Eryri lily in her palm, then leaned forward and kissed her lips. She held back, and he knew she did it out of respect for his preferences for privacy. And for that, he loved her all the more. He caressed her cheek with his thumb while staring into her eyes, the cheers of his warband failing to bother him this time. She was a quick study. She followed Rigana's example and ushered him toward Gwynafar on her left.

Instead of smiling as the others had, Gwynafar stood tall and stoic, an icy edge to her features that would have been more fitting out in the blizzard than in a cozy feasting hall. But he knew what Eilinor expected, so he performed his duties without hesitation.

"Gwynafar, third of my wives." Arthur held out the third flower with the bright yellow petals, but she did not take it immediately. She stared coldly into his eyes for several seconds before finally glancing down at his offering. Her eyes went wide with shock and her face paled.

She swallowed and shook her head.

Arthur took her gently by the hand, opened her limp palm, and placed the flower in it before closing her fingers around it. He steeled himself and leaned down to kiss her. Gwynafar recoiled and held up the flower.

"How did you know?" She hissed the words in a whisper, glaring at him as she pushed the flower in his face.

Eilinor appeared suddenly beside them, mischief glinting in her green eyes. "Is there a problem with your husband's gift, Lady Gwynafar?"

Gwynafar turned on the witch queen. "Do you mock me, crone?"

Her gaze flicked toward Lanslot.

Rigana bolted sideways, reaching her arms out toward Gwyanafar, but Talara was just as fast, catching her around the waist and pushing her back. "No, sister!"

Gwynafar scoffed, and fiery anger rolled like waves through Arthur's body. He clenched his fists to his sides, sure this was some test of his patience. "You will give our hostess all the respect she is due."

His third wife smiled mockingly at him. "Why, of course, Dux Bellorum! As soon as the witch gives her respect to me."

He'd never considered hitting a woman off the field of battle, but he barely suppressed the urge to lash out.

Eilinor, still smiling, placed a steady hand on Arthur's chest and walked between him and Gwynafar. "She does not like your golden gift, Arturius. It is her gift nonetheless, to love or to hate."

"Yes, lady," he grounded out through gritted teeth.

She turned deadly fast to Gwynafar, and her smile tightened. There was no longer any warmth in her eyes. "But as a lady born of a certain station in life, you still have your duties. If you choose to abandon those duties, you will suffer the consequences."

The last sentence sounded more like a threat than an observation, but Arthur didn't bother objecting. Gwynafar could use a dose of fear to get her skinny ass in line.

"Wives of Arturius," Eilinor called, clapping her hands sharply. The hall fell into silence around them. "And the great war chief himself... Follow me"

She wove through the tables, Arthur and his wives following her like ducklings to their mother, and brought them to the central hearth where a black iron cauldron hung over the fire. Talara held Rigana's hand, and Arthur noticed she squeezed it as they arranged themselves around the cauldron.

All the witches and warriors in the hall watched, some sipping their mead, others nibbling at the herbed breads and perfectly roasted meats.

"Arturius," Eilinor spoke loudly as she approached him. "I need a lock of your hair."

"It is yours, lady," he said firmly, and she drew a knife from some hidden pocket in her robes, wasting no time in cutting a thick lock from his head.

She tossed it into the cauldron and picked up the ladle to stir it. "A drop of the moon's light," she called in a sing-song voice, and one of her witches brought her a vial of iridescent white liquid. A single, precious drop was added before the glass vial was stoppered again.

After stirring the cauldron gently, she called out a succession of ingredients, her witches waiting in a predetermined line to deliver them. "Silver Fumes, those from the Fire of the Ancients. Ash from the sacred grove. Dragon's blood resin, and dragon's claw root."

Plop. Splash. Kerplunk.

"Water from the cauldron of our great goddess Ceridwen." The tiniest drop of water from a metal vial was added to Eilinor's cauldron. "And finally... your wives."

Arthur felt his heart stop in the silence, and his head snapped toward the witch queen.

"Oh, don't be barbaric." She waved a hand as if she hadn't imagined her words could be taken in such a way. "They need to offer their gifts from you into the cauldron."

"And what are you making, Lady Eilinor?" Rigana asked, leaning forward to look into the magic waters.

"Back! Stay back, good wife of Arturius!" Eilinor ushered her backward. "Not a drop can be spilled, and no one may drink this potion but your husband."

Rigana arched a fiery eyebrow and glanced at Arthur. He nodded, and they shared that knowing look, communicating his trust of the witch and Rigana's trust of him without a word spoken.

"All that is mine to give, I give to ensure the victory of my husband, my greatest friend, my love." And she held forward the purple flower Arthur had given her.

"Drop it in," Eilinor instructed, nodding her head toward the concoction.

Rigana let the purple flower fall into the cauldron, flinching back as it bubbled.

"Ah! A wonderful sign. Your heart and your words are true, Rigana," the witch said, laughing warmly. "But everyone already knew that. Your turn, Talara."

His warriors crowded in closer now, watching intently as the ritual neared its end.

"What will this potion do to him?" Talara asked, pinning the witch with a suspicious gaze.

"This will help your husband stop the white dragon and win the war to save your people."

"Will it... do something to me?"

"Very perceptive. You've studied with the druids, haven't you?"

Talara nodded toward Arthur. "Until he won my hand."

"You trust him?"

Relaxing, Talara nodded. "I do."

"And you are happy to have your fate bound with his?"

Arthur's chest pinched at her words, the night at the riverside flashing in his mind's eye. He almost wanted to tell her to take her flower and run, but he forced himself to be rational. Everything would happen as it was supposed to, and she would be okay. He knew it.

A sudden smile warmed Talara's worried face. "I've already promised that, Eilinor, and I stand by it still."

She tossed the lily into the cauldron, and a soft white light flared and lingered in the cauldron. Eilinor gasped in delight, stirring it gently. "Your love is deep and true, Talara. The love you share with this man transcends lifetimes. I see your spirals intertwined and unending."

Talara's eyes welled with tears, and she bit her bottom lip. Arthur wished he could hold her, comfort her, and take joy in that news with her, but he resisted. They would all celebrate when he could sit down to feast with his people.

"Gwynafar," Eilinor called, her voice sweet as honey. "It's your turn."

But Gwynafar's face had turned ghostly pale, and her body trembled violently as she stared at the cauldron with tears welling in her eyes. "I... can't..."

The words were so soft Arthur barely heard them, but they had formed clearly on her lips.

"What was that, lady?" Eilinor asked, voice raised as she rounded the cauldron and stood next to Gwynafar.

"I cannot," Gwynafar repeated loudly, trembling as she lifted her chin.

Arthur wasn't surprised at her answer, but he was surprised that she had stopped pretending in front of the rest of his people. He crossed his arms over his chest and glanced at Eilinor, but her eyes told him to wait.

Tears streamed down Gwynafar's face, and she refused to look at anyone, staring instead in the rafters.

"Your fate is already bound to Arturius, Gwynafar. This," Eilinor gestured to the cauldron, "is merely an affirmation of the promise you already made."

Tension filled the space between the words, Arthur's nerves on edge, until the witch queen prodded again. "Would you break your oath and bind yourself to another?"

Gwynafar's face turned red as she glared daggers at Eilinor. "I don't know what you mean."

"To the one who's already given you the yellow flower. You've given your love—"

"Shut up!" Gwynafar screamed and hurled herself at Eilinor.

Arthur, Talara, and Rigana all bolted forward and grabbed Gwynafar's arms, preventing her from striking the witch queen and hauling her away from the woman.

"Let me go!" she screeched, twisting and writhing until they released her.

"How dare you attack the woman who saved our lives?" Arthur boomed, keeping himself between the women.

His warriors cowered, and Gwynafar flinched. Arthrur's vision blurred for a moment, but he shook it off. It was a feeling he hadn't experienced since his visit to Calleva.

"She is tricking us, husband! Sh-she wishes to turn you further against me." She whirled, searching the faces of his warriors before shouting as she fled to the far side of the roundhouse. "This is all a trap to bring me to ruin and to kill my husband! Raise up your weapons and stop her!"

The women in Arthur's warband variously rolled their eyes or looked to him for guidance. But to Arthur's shock, every man who'd sworn him their loyalty readied sword, spear, and dagger as they began stalking toward the witch queen.

Beg for Mercy

ARTHUR CLENCHED HIS FISTS. "You will stop!"

The men cringed briefly at his booming voice, but then resumed their march for the witch queen.

"They are under her spell, Arturius!" Eilinor warned him, her voice distressed in a way he wouldn't have imagined was possible.

"How do I break it?" he asked before punching one of his men in the face, sending him flying backward. He landed on his back with a thud but rose quickly, blood pouring from his nose. His glassy eyes looked right through Arthur.

"She must be bound! My acolytes will assist you." The witches huddled in a corner behind their table on the raised platform, holding hands. Their whispered chants sounded like a pit of snakes hissing and slithering.

"Arthur!" Myrddin called, jumping down from the platform with his staff raised. "I can help—"

One of Arthur's warriors smashed a fist into the side of the bard's head as he ran, sending him smashing face-first into the floor. He did not move. Arthur swallowed the urge to run to his side, instead looking between Gwynafar and the witch. His men were closing fast in the limited space, and the witch was backed against a wall now, surrounded. All that stood between the witch and a dozen blades glinting with firelight were Talara and Rigana.

"Aelwen, Dara!" he called, summoning the woman Drystan had been spending so much time with lately and the other of his warrior women standing beside her. "Knock them out! Save the witch queen and try not to kill our men."

"You must hurry, friends of Arturius. You, the greatest of men, must stop the witch from hurting me and killing your king!" Gwynafar cried out to Arthur's bewitched warriors, and they obeyed, picking up their feet and scurrying toward where the witch queen was cornered with only two protectors.

Arthur threw fists and elbows as he pushed through the men and sprinted between the tables toward Gwynafar. Her eyes grew wide with fear as he approached, but something struck his head, filling his vision with white as the pain rang through his skull. He found himself on the floor. His vision blurred from the blow landed on him, but he scrambled until he righted himself and stood, grabbing a chair for support. Pressing one hand to his head where it throbbed, he pulled it away and saw red. His hand was covered in blood.

His blood dripped from his fingers and splattered on the floor.

When Arthur looked up toward Gwynafar, Lanslot stood in the way. "You?"

"You are not yourself, Arthur," Lanslot said, standing tall and drawing his shoulders back proudly. "You have forgotten that this lady is your wife. She deserves your deepest respect, admiration, and love, all of which you have denied her from the very beginning."

"Do you hear yourself, Lanslot? She has bewitched you!" The throb of a muted ache pressed against his skull, and he tried to resist letting it distract him.

"You are the one enspelled," he nodded toward the witch queen, "by that woman and her wicked acolytes."

"I can forgive you," Arthur offered, "if you move out of the way now. Honor your oaths to me and to our people, and help me subdue Gwynafar. You must break her hold over your mind!"

Lanslot's eyes hardened, and one hand crept towards the sword on his hip. He drew the blade, the metal singing lightly above as it left the scabbard. "I am thinking clearly, Arthur, and with honor in my heart."

Arthur could hear the women fighting off the entranced men. Grunting, smacking, thudding, then a woman's cry. He was desperate to look, to know that they were holding their own, but he didn't dare take his gaze from Lanslot. There was no fighting a sword with his fists, so he drew Excalibur from his scabbard and held the sword aloft.

"You would fight your oldest friend at the behest of a witch?" Lanslot scowled and tightened his grip.

"I would ask the same of you!" Arthur roared and sprang forward with a wide swing aimed for Lanslot's throat, but the man was fast, and he blocked with his sword. The blades crashed together, and they pushed their weight bodily against each other, the blades ringing until the hilts tangled.

Lanslot broke away and retreated backward, readying his sword to block again. They had been sparring partners for more than a decade, and they knew each other's moves better than anyone else. But Arthur had the advantage in height and weight, and he was confident he could wear the smaller man down. Just behind Lanslot, Gwynafar stood grinning even as she pressed herself against the far wall.

A rage sparked in Arthur then, for all the frustration and pain she had wrought since he'd first arrived in Calleva, and he burst forward with his sword raised. He stabbed, slashed, and swung blow after blow at Lanslot, the self-elected champion of his monster of a wife. Lanslot blocked blow after blow, but they were coming too fast for him to counter. Arthur crashed the blows down on him, one after another, aiming to cleave the man's skull with Excalibur.

The anger fueling his rage tunneled his vision, so he saw only Lanslot, the sweat trickling down his face, the tremor in his hands as he blocked another blow, the true terror now ruining the man's once fearless eyes.

"How could you betray me?!" Arthur roared, each word delivered in staccato and accompanied by a bone-shaking blow of his sword.

Lanslot backed into a table and stumbled sideways, tangling himself in a chair, and his sword slipped from his fingers, clattering to the hard earthen floor of the roundhouse. He landed on his back and held his hands up to defend himself as Arthur pulled back his enchanted blade for the final swing at Lanslot's face.

A blur of white entered his vision as Gwynafar threw herself on top of Lanslot and screamed, "Stop!"

Arthur barely halted the blade, unsure why he'd listened. He'd rather be done with them both at once, but some unseen force muddied his mind. She held up one delicate hand, tears trickling down her cheeks, and she stared up at him with those sparkling blue eyes.

"Please, Arthur. Let us go. I beg for your mercy. Let us leave this place and our presence will plague you no more."

He thought about it for half a heartbeat. "No."

But as he raised his sword up to swing, she shouted out a warning. "Let us go, or they'll all die."

There were no tears in her eyes now as she pointed past him.

He turned slowly to find the witch queen, his wives, and the other two women warriors kneeling on the ground. His entranced warriors stood behind them, blade tips pressed to the backs of the women's unprotected necks.

Arthur's hand trembled so violently that he nearly dropped his blade. "Let them go. All of them!"

She smiled up at him. "As soon as we're out that door, I'll release them all."

He growled and chopped his sword through the empty air in frustration. "Pick up your puppet and leave then!"

Gwynafar's satisfied smile only added to his fury, but he knew the stakes, so he could only watch as Lanslot retrieved his sword and limped toward the door while leaning against Gwynafar for support. When they disappeared through the doorway, the pounding in Arthur's head faded. He sprinted toward his people, waiting for the enchantment to release his men.

They all took in a breath together, their weapons still raised and pointed at the kneeling women.

"Drystan," Aelwen said with a trembling voice.

"No!" Arthur cried out, and in a last-ditch effort to save someone, he hurled his sword at an enemy he never expected to face: his own friends.

"Please don't—" Aelwen's final words were cut off as Drystan drove his spear through her back and twisted it into her spine.

Arthur's spatha spun through the air until it cleaved into the faces of three men, stopping their intended attack on the witch queen and Rigana. The men behind Dara plunged their swords into her neck and skull, killing her instantly.

Talara threw herself forward as the spearmen behind her thrust downward with their weapons, but one blade pierced her through the calf and pinned her to the earth so she couldn't crawl away. As she screamed in pain, Arthur leapt through the air and threw himself into the two spearmen, smashing their bodies backward. They did not cry out in pain, did not groan, did not utter a single word. As

Arthur scrambled up, they fought to grasp their spears, and when one managed to get hold of his, he pinned his dead-eyed gaze on Talara again.

She groaned as she tried to pull the spear out of the ground, but she had no leverage, and with every movement of the spear, new cries of pain escaped her throat.

Arthur grabbed the spearman around the waist and hurled him backward, his head smashing into the wall behind them. His body went limp, so Arthur dropped him and took his spear as the other spearman hovered over Talara and raised his spear. Bursting forward, Arthur impaled the warrior through the spine in the center of his back, and the spear fell harmlessly to the side.

Beside him, Rigana had taken up Excalibur and used it to kill the rest of the men.

Only Drystan remained, sobbing and moaning as he rocked back and forth, Aelwen's bloody body limp in his arms. "No! By the gods, please no!"

Lightning and Fire

ARTHUR WATCHED A WITCH in light green robes visibly sweating as she held a ceramic vial over the cauldron. Eilinor stirred the liquid one more time before scooping a spoonful of it and expertly dripping it into the vial.

"But that little bitch didn't put her flower in," Rigana half-growled. "Will this potion still work?"

"I never needed her flower." Eilinor gently hooked the ladle on the bar over the cauldron and plucked a cork from a hidden pocket in her robes. "From the moment you arrived, I knew she held no loyalty or love for Arthur. One cannot participate in that ritual if the truth of their intentions remains hidden."

"So what was the purpose?" Myrddin asked, still pressing a blood-soaked cloth against his head. Beside him, a blue-robed witch applied a poultice of healing herbs to the hole in Talara's leg while she gritted her teeth and squeezed her eyes shut.

"To bring what was hidden to the light before it could spoil all of our careful planning. And Arthur had to prove he could be my champion," Eilinor answered as she ensured the stopper was stuck tight. "Clearly, he achieved that when he faced Lanslot and struck down his own men to save me."

Arthur didn't want to be reminded of the dead men, though their bodies lay in a neat row along the wall only a few strides from where he now sat.

Eilinor passed the vial to Rigana and folded the younger woman's hands around it. "I am sorry, Rigana, that this is your burden to carry."

When the witch's hands slipped away, Rigana lifted the vial gingerly and held it away from her face as she inspected it, as if the tiny container might spontaneously combust at any second. "It seems a small thing to carry for Arthur. Do I need to force him to drink it?"

The witch grinned wryly and shook her head. "No. But you are the only one who will know when to give it to him." She turned to lock eyes with Arthur. "And when she does, you must drink all of it, Dux Bellorum. Immediately."

He nodded solemnly, pretending not to be distracted by Drystan still sitting in his periphery, holding Aelwen's stiffening corpse. The big man didn't have any tears left in him, but he continued to mourn without them, and Arthur did not begrudge him that. He remembered with shame how he'd pushed Myrddin to continue forward after the death of Anieras and vowed he wouldn't make the same mistake with Drystan.

"Swear you will drink it when you are ready to call the dragon."

"I swear it, Lady Eilinor." He bowed his head in deference, then returned to cleaning the blood and bits of flesh clinging to Excalibur's blade and hilt. "But I fear we're out of time. From what you've described, we're in the farthest reaches of the mountains of Cymru, and the Saxons with their dragon are in the east, likely marching on Londinium as we speak. It could take us a week to get there."

She shook her head and tsked as she assisted with Talara's healing. "You have a few hours yet. You simply won't have the time to move slowly once you arrive."

"I have no intention of moving slowly," he grumbled, sheathing his sword before fixing his gaze on the cooling bodies of the men who had entrusted him with their lives. "None whatsoever."

"How long do we have until dawn?" Rigana asked as she grabbed a new cloth for Myrddin and took the bloody one from him.

"A few hours."

Arthur's teeth clenched. Time continued to slip away, lost to unnecessary tragedies, and the moment he would face the white dragon was nearly upon him.

"We need to leave, Eilinor," Arthur said. "I do not mean to hurry away—"

"You have fulfilled your quest, Arturius. Every step has been completed. You earned the golden eagle." She pointed to the standard leaning against the wall near the far entrance. "Viviane gave you the gift of wisdom and blessed your sword. And I give you the potion, the last piece of the puzzle. Although, there is something Anieras didn't convey correctly."

Myrddin perked up, instantly on the defensive for his grandfather. "He said that I needed the eagle feathers," he pointed to his staff where they hung, "to help Arthur."

"Correct. Do you know how? Did he give you any hint?"

"Well, no."

She nodded. "One feather is for you, and one is for Arturius. The third will remain on your staff. You must first paint the duir on each other's hands."

"The oak tree," Arthur observed. It was a powerful symbol.

She continued, "Then you will each keep your feather around your neck."

"A binding?" Myrddin asked, and Arthur stiffened.

"Yes, bard. It is indeed." She turned her gaze on Arthur, as if she could hear his thoughts. "Sometimes the friends we make later in life are the ones that stay with us in the hardest of times. You will bind yourself with Myrddin, or you will have come all this way only to fail."

He swallowed his protests and nodded. "Please lead us, lady."

The symbols were painted in charcoal on the back of each man's dominant hand, then prayed over in the language of the druids by Eilinor. Arthur felt as if a loose thread within him had been pulled taut, stretching from somewhere deep within his core to his hand, and from his hand to Myrddin's.

"Now hurry!" Eilinor gestured toward the door.

"I can go too," Talara said, pushing to her feet and cringing with every step as she limped toward Arthur, Myrddin, and Rigana.

"No, hearth sister," Rigana said, brushing a hand over Talara's hair. "I will watch over our husband. You must focus on your healing so you can return to us swiftly."

Talara took Rigana's hand from her face and squeezed it, worry etched in the lines of her face and glistening in her eyes. "You can't go without me. I just have this feeling that I need to be there."

"I would feel the same in your position," Rigana assured her. "But if you insist on coming instead of staying here to heal, then we'll be forced to look after you instead of fight."

That seemed to sink in as Talara nodded and lowered herself into a seat. "Look out for each other, all right? For me?"

"Of course, beloved," Arthur said. "We'll meet again soon."

He looked to see if Drystan would join them, but found the man hadn't moved at all. As they followed Lady Eilinor and walked past him, Arthur stopped to place a hand on his shoulder and crouched down beside him. "I'm sorry, Drystan. We all know she loved you."

Drystan raised one cold hand and briefly placed it on Arthur's. Then he lifted it and returned his attention to Aelwen, smoothing the hair back from her blood-splattered face. He never said a word, even as what remained of Arthur's warband left the roundhouse without him.

A full moon hung low in the clear night sky, falling toward the horizon with the late hour. The blizzard had ended some hours ago, and the freezing air was still. White clouds puffed in front of them with each breath as they made their way out of the village and down to the ridge where the ritual circle lay dark and silent. As Arthur walked beside Lady Eilinor, he noticed that the path they followed already held two sets of footprints through the otherwise unmarred snowy landscape.

Gwynafar and Lanslot.

"They're waiting for us," he whispered to the witch queen.

"Perhaps."

"Should we—"

"You must focus, Arthur. All you can do is be prepared. Expect to see them so you are not surprised."

"That is a simple thing to say."

"And a harder thing to do, I know."

The footprints through the snow ended at the ritual circle, but Arthur reached the circle without incident and found no other trace of the traitors.

Eilinor led them into the center, arranged them in a triangle, and then walked around and pressed the palm of her left hand to each wooden post of the circle. When she had finished, she exited the ritual circle and lifted her arms overhead, palms and face skyward, as she whispered her magic into the heavens.

"Good luck, you three. Remember to give him the potion, Rigana." She held up one hand in farewell, her carefree eyes touched with a hint of sadness.

A sizzle made Arthur flinch, reminding him painfully of being struck by the bolt when he'd first approached the ritual circle. Lightning arced between the posts, their inscriptions glowing blue and pulsing with a rhythm that matched his heartbeat. They throbbed faster and faster; the lightning growing fiercer and brighter, and he squeezed the hands of his friend and his wife tighter and tighter until a final blast erupted.

All was silent for several heartbeats. Arthur could hear nothing, see nothing, smell nothing, taste nothing. He barely felt Myrddin and Rigana's hands clasped in his own.

Then sounds exploded in his ears again—horses hooves thundering across the ground, the war cries of men, the screams of people being cut down. He smelled something burning, tasted the tang of fresh blood in the air. When he opened his eyes, he found he was in the center of a circle of ancient standing stones.

He wanted to smile at Rigana, and share his astonishment with Myrddin, but they were already deep in the chaos of battle. People screamed and fought all around them, few taking notice of their sudden appearance, and few having the luxury of turning to look without getting skewered by their opponent.

A rumbling sound shook the earth, and Myrddin and Rigana's faces twisted in horror as they stared over Arthur's head. Halfway across the battlefield, a white dragon with leathery wings leapt into the air, glided down into a mass of tribal warriors, and tore them to shreds with its teeth and talons.

Rigana screamed.

Arthur tore his gaze away from the dragon to find Rigana being held, head pulled back by her hair and a dagger across her throat. He froze, recognizing the delicate hand that held the weapon.

The woman peered around Rigana's tall shoulder. "Hello, husband."

Gwynafar kicked Rigana behind the knee, making her fall hard to the ground, the dagger slicing a thin cut into her neck. Blood dripped in a small trail over Rigana's clavicle and into her tunic. Her green eyes blazed fiercely without a hint of fear, but as brave as she was, even she knew when she was at a disadvantage.

"Myrddin—"

"Right here, Arthur," Myrddin said, his voice quivering.

Lanslot stood behind the bard, the tip of his sword resting against Myrddin's back. "Give me the potion, Arthur."

Call the Dragon

ARTHUR'S HEART POUNDED IN his ears as his gaze flicked between Gwynafar and Lanslot.

"How could you betray me like this?" he demanded, glaring at Lanslot.

"You are a slave to the old gods and their puppets. I never let myself see it until Gwynafar forced me to open my eyes."

Yes. He thought back to a time that felt like it was years in the past and accepted that he should have left her on the Via Augusta outside of Calleva. So many lives could have been spared.

"If you can't even take care of one beautiful, loving, gentle lady, how could you possibly be trusted with the survival of all the tribes against the Saxons?"

Wind stirred in the circle as Arthur weighed his options. He tried not to look at Rigana, forced himself not to even glance at her belt where the vial hung in a leather pouch. He watched from his periphery as her deft fingers silently worked the pouch open.

"There is a battle raging all around us, and your only thought is of this woman?" Arthur laughed. "Oh, Lanslot. How you've fallen. From brave warrior to smitten boy."

Lanslot's face burned red, his eyes hard as he glared at Arthur. "Say it again," he prodded, grabbing Myrddin by the shoulder and flexing the muscles in his sword arm. "We'll see if the bard has enough magic to survive my sword."

"Arthur!" Rigana called, and she flung the vial at him.

He barely looked in time to see the small, ceramic container flying toward him. Leaping forward, he caught it with one hand just before it would have slammed into the stone floor of the ritual circle and shattered. Smiling in relief, he looked at Rigana, who stumbled forward, clutching her neck.

Black blood pulsed from her throat, spurting and bubbling from the deep wound. Arthur scrambled toward her, a guttural scream escaping his throat, but a blast of lightning arced through the ritual circle, striking everyone inside the stones. He lay on his back for several seconds, stunned, fighting for dominion over his limbs.

When he finally could move again, he rolled onto his stomach and crawled to Rigana, turning her onto her back. The blood loss had slowed now, but the light dimmed in her eyes. Tears dripped into the bloody mess on her neck, and Arthur realized he was crying. He kissed her forehead and held her close as her pulse slowed, then felt her spirit caress his face one final time as she died.

"Drink the potion!" Myrddin cried out as he stumbled to his feet.

He didn't remember dropping the vial, but his hands were empty.

Numbing himself to his grief, he gently laid Rigana on the smooth stone slab, then began searching for the vial, scurrying and slipping in the spreading pool of his first wife's warm blood. He spotted it lodged in a broken crevice of the floor just as Lanslot climbed to his feet and reached for his sword.

Arthur yanked the cork from the vial, exhaled, and then downed every drop of the potion. It burned like boiling water and spices, bitter and acidic, and he cried out as it burned all the way down. He dropped to his knees, holding his stomach, skin burning and sweating as the potion boiled and burbled within him. Falling on his side as pins and needles flooded every inch of his skin, he watched helplessly as Myrddin fought Lanslot.

From out of nowhere, Drystan appeared and charged Lanslot from the side, bowling him over before drawing his sword, then squaring off with the man when Lanslot got to his feet again. Arthur looked around for Gwynafar, sure she would be on top of him any moment to finish the job, but saw Talara half-crouched and walking in a slow circle with Gywnafar, holding Excalibur ready to strike.

Myrddin dropped beside Arthur and pressed a hand to his forehead, then reeled back and shook his hand. "Can you hear me?"

His voice was muted, as if Arthur heard him from underwater. He wanted to nod his head, but his body convulsed, and he had lost control over it again. Myrddin suddenly glanced sideways and barely dodged an attack from Lanslot by throwing himself into the grass outside the circle.

Arthur wanted to see what was happening, where Drystan had gone, and to hopefully find Talara standing over Gwynafar's fresh corpse, but he could only writhe on the cold stone slabs. New bolts of pain raced through his bones, stretching and pulling and breaking in a hundred places all at once. Someone let out a blood-curdling scream, and it took Arthur a moment to realize that it had been him. It didn't sound like a voice he recognized. The screaming twisted and burst anew as the terrible agony of his body crushed his spirit.

Grief, love, worry, desire, friendship, and hatred all turned numb in his mind as rage consumed him. Rage from the physical and emotional pain of all he'd been through fueled him as his limbs transformed, legs breaking backward, and wings bursting from his back. His skin stretched and tore and healed over and over as the change rippled through him.

When he looked down, his hands were as red as fire, and long black talons emerged from where his fingernails had once been. He was vaguely aware of his human self, hidden somewhere in the back of his mind, reminding him of the words of the gods, ghosts, and witches: he would call the dragon on the dawn of the seventh day.

The rising dawn lit the sky in a fury of red, amber, and purple hues, and Arturius felt he was seeing these colors more vibrantly than he ever had before. Everything was clear. He saw eagles flying high above the earth so clearly that he watched their feathers twitch against the wind currents.

"Arturius!" a voice called out, echoing in his mind. This was someone important he knew, and someone, he quickly decided, that he should be careful not to eat.

He swung his giant head down to peer at the small creature calling him.

"Myrddin," he said, but the deep, rumbling growl of his voice surprised him. He liked it very much.

"Save Talara!" Myrddin shouted.

The name sparked some strange feeling of familiarity, a feeling of calm and cozy warmth within, but he didn't know why. Human Arthur, who had been pushed to the back of his mind, was trying to tell him what the name meant, but Arturius couldn't hear what he was saying.

Myrddin pointed his beautifully carved staff toward something, but Arturius was distracted by the shiny thing on top. It sparkled, catching his eye, and he felt compelled to take the sparkly stone and hide it.

"No! You idiot!" Myrddin swung his staff out of Arturius's reach. "Go get Gwynafar!"

That name sent a spear of fresh rage boiling through his veins, and he whipped his head around to find a blonde human in a white dress splattered with blood. Her chest heaved and her body trembled as she stumbled backward, tripping on a cracked slab.

Magic flowed through this one, a dark red aura winding around her like tangled roots. Their ends lashed out, whipping at him, but he was too strong now. He could feel the lingering protection of Mars Rigisamus over Arthur and understood that the shield had dulled the pain of her attacks, even though it couldn't stop them altogether. But against Arturius, the Red Dragon, she was no more successful than a fruit fly attacking a tree.

He knew with a single look that, whether as a dragon or human, he hated this creature. She said something, but he couldn't hear her past his own rumbling as he focused on her. Crawling to her knees, she clasped her hands together and held them before her, tears streaming down her cheeks as she appeared to plead with him.

Arturius was not moved by this gesture.

The blonde one's eyes shot wide open when he growled, then sucked in a breath. He blew it out, and flames engulfed her frail body. She screamed in misery, hysterical as the fire consumed her. Reaching out a claw, he snatched her up and clamped his teeth down on her head.

A piercing pain caused him to cry out, bits of the blonde one's flesh still hanging from his teeth, and he shied from the pain, looking to see what had done him harm. It was another human. Recognition of this one brought more pain to his soul than his body, despite the bastard stabbing and swinging that bloody sword around. Arturius reared back his head, and bit down on the man when he pulled back for another swing, severing him at the hips. The sword fell from his twitching hand and clattered to the ground as Arturius chewed through bone and sinew before swallowing his meal.

The food repaired him, his wounds healing before his very eyes, and re-sparked the fiery rage within him. He would have continued eating the rest of the swordsman, but a roar resounded behind him, and he turned to face it.

A white dragon approached with an army of blood-soaked, trembling Saxons. He roared loudly, boasting of battles won, his magnificent wings, and his great hoard of treasure.

Dominion of the Sky

ARTURIUS FOLDED HIS WINGS in and stalked forward, studying the braggart's many old scars and fresh wounds. He also noticed a limp in one of his front legs.

"And who," the white dragon rumbled each elongated syllable in his deep breathy voice, "are you?"

"Arturiusssss," he hissed his reply, his tongue clumsy in this new language.

"I am Rrrrhaegar," he said, the first syllable rolling violently through his deeply stained teeth. "You will join me, young dragon, or you will die."

Giving a toothy smile as his only warning, Arturius flared his wings open and leapt forward, snapping his jaws on Rhaegar's front left leg. The older dragon bellowed in pain and jumped back, but Arturius sunk his fangs in deeper and held on tight, tumbling and rolling with Rhaegar as he flailed. Their bodies slammed onto the ground, crushing men beneath them.

A flurry of wings stirred up giant clouds of dust, and their tails whipping frantically back and forth tore the legs from under the men who couldn't get out of the way fast enough. Snapping teeth, needling talons, and bone-grinding strength brought the beasts together in a battle royale for the ages. Arturius scrambled, tearing his talons across Rhaegar's slick scales, and rearing his head back to snap his teeth into the other leg.

Rhaegar howled in pain again before striking downward and snapping his teeth into Arturius's neck. The searing pain nearly paralyzed Arthur, and he released the other leg before flailing to get away. He rolled, crushing several men, then sucked in a deep breath and spewed a stream of liquid fire on Rhaegar. When the stream died and Arturius was left panting and trembling, Rhaegar still stood, body shaking with thunderous laughter.

"Fire does not hurt usss," Rhaegar said through his laughter. "Save it to char your dinner."

Rheagar launched himself into the sky, the downwash from his white wings sending men tumbling away. Arturius watched, grumbling deep in his chest as he flexed his wings. He followed Rhaegar's example, bending his legs, then jumping up into the sky. It took him a few tries to get off the ground, but when he finally did, flight came naturally. He soared into the air, seeking his rival, and savoring the caress of the wind over his scales.

I know how to beat him, a voice said, but Arturius heard the words in his mind rather than with his ears. It was the human man, the one close to his heart. Oh, yes. Myrddin.

Then tell me, he thought back grumpily, focusing as his eyes searched the clouds for Rhaegar.

Bring him back to the ritual circle.

The what?

He heard a mental sigh from Myrddin. *The great circle of standing stones. It holds the magic of the land. I can help you if you bring him here, and we can defeat him together.*

You don't get all the glory, wizard.

I'm not a wizard, Arthur.

Arthur isn't here, idiot human. Arturius is in charge now, and if you disrespect me, I'll eat you for dinner. He wasn't really going to eat Myrddin, but it didn't hurt to scare some respect into the frail creature.

He is faster and stronger than you, Arturius. He's been doing this longer than you have, and he has all the advantages. Bring him down here so I can give you an edge.

Hmmmm, he sent a grumbling thought through their link. *I don't know.*

Do you remember Excalibur?

The name excited him, sending a bolt of energy through his aching body. *I think I do!*

Excalibur wants to taste the blood of the white dragon, but you'll need to bring him down here.

Bah! Fine. Arturius took a deep breath, then wildly blasted the clouds with fire. One of the gray-white shapes didn't evaporate. It was the white dragon.

Getting used to his wings now, Arturius burst forward and gave chase to Rhaegar. They spun, twisted, and tumbled through the clouds, soaring, then diving hard, only to soar again.

His soul buzzed with joy as they chased each other, and Arturius could bear no malice toward Rhaegar up here. This was their dominion, their freedom, their truest joy. The wars of men couldn't reach them here, and he felt that burden falling like shredded scales from his strong shoulders.

Stop playing, you fool! We... we need to prepare Rigana for Annwn. We need to bury her.

The human soul within him tore at himself, wailing at Myrddin's words. Something about them had stolen all the joy from Arturius's flight, too. He had the knowledge of loving Rigana, even if he didn't have the memories within him. That love sprang from his soul, not from the memories and instincts of this vessel.

"Rigana," he rumbled her name into the sky and quickly sobered. He remembered why he needed to get Rhaegar to the ground, so he swerved through the clouds searching for him. "How do you fly so high, old one?"

"I'm not old!" Rhaegar snapped.

Arturius let out booming laughter that echoed through the skies. "Old and slow." He pretended to yawn as he glided through the sky around Rhaegar. "Your wings were glorious once, but they are frail now."

That lit a fire in the white dragon, and he beat his wings in massive strokes as he bolted after Arturius.

Folding in his wings, Arturius dove toward the earth, the wind tearing at the edges of his wings as the ground flew up to meet him. He opened his wings at the last second, just above the ritual circle, but he'd timed it too late. He hit the ground and slid through the forest, leaving a massive ditch in his wake.

Rhaegar bellowed his laughter, landing gracefully next to Arturius's still form. "You are funny, young one. I will give you one more chance to join me."

Arturius lifted his pounding head, his neck aching, and bared his teeth. He gathered his feet under himself and leapt into the sky, wobbling on his sore wings as he searched for the circle of stones. Just as he spotted it, a rush of air warned Arturius that Rhaegar was just above him. Twisting in the air, he hooked the talons of all four of his feet into the white dragon's legs and sides.

Rhaegar screamed as he fought to keep them above the ground, batting his wings hard, but he wasn't strong enough to carry them both. They crashed into a copse of trees, rolling and tumbling together until they emerged in the clearing next to the ritual circle. Arturius saw double when he opened his eyes, squirming and struggling to untangle his body from Rhaegar's limp, groaning form.

Hurry! Get him into the circle!

Shut up, Myrddin! Arturius shook his serpentine head, trying to clear his vision. Rhaegar was moving again, so he studied the distance between the older dragon and the circle. His neck still ached from where Rhaegar had latched onto him, and he swiped at it with one sore claw. *Ah-ha!*

After stretching his jaw, Arturius opened his maw as wide as he could, then snapped it down on Rhaegar's neck. The dragon woke, bellowing in pain. He tried to claw and beat his wings, but just as he had done to Arturius, Arturius had nearly paralyzed him by biting the white dragon's neck. With all the energy he'd gained from eating those first two humans, Arturius walked backward on his four strong legs and dragged Rhaegar along with him.

Occasionally, the older dragon would shake and writhe, but Arturius's bite was too powerful, clamping against his spine in a way that drained his strength.

"Lay his head in the circle!" Myrddin commanded.

Arturius grumbled but did as the human asked—this time, anyway. He could threaten him again later, he supposed. He twisted Rhaegar by the neck, weaving his thick, massive body between the stones, then pinning the heavy-breathing beast's head in the center.

Hurry, Arturius grumbled mentally to Myrddin. *He's regaining his strength.*

Myrddin began chanting, and a woman's voice joined in. Something sparked in Arturius. It felt sweet and hopeful, like... love?

Rhaegar growled, lashing out with his taloned feet at Myrddin, but the human deftly dodged the attempt and moved on quickly, drawing the duir symbol on each of the stones with a hand covered in ash. On the opposite side of the circle, the woman did the same.

A group of warriors began converging on their location as the voices of Myrddin and the woman rose in a crescendo of power, calling the gods to aid them in binding the white dragon.

"We've got him, Arturius," Myrddin shouted over the sudden gale. "Keep the warriors away from us!"

Reluctantly, Arturius opened his sore jaw and dropped Rhaegar's head in the center of the circle. The older dragon's limbs and tail twitched, but he could not move.

"I hate druids! Don't do this, young one. There are many things I could teach you. I... I could join you."

"No!" Myrddin shouted, slamming his staff into the stone floor of the ritual circle. "I can see your heart, son of Hengist. You are ruthless and cruel, and you have betrayed everyone who has trusted you."

Arturius didn't hold that against him, but he was bound to Myrddin, so he turned toward the oncoming warriors and left the circle. He hauled back his head, sucked in air, then opened his aching jaw and set the warriors to flame. When nothing moved, he returned his gaze to the circle and watched Myrddin perform his ritual, speaking in the old tongues that seemed familiar to Arturius.

The dark-haired creature, glowing with beauty of mind and spirit, approached Rhaegar's head with a sword held firmly in her hands. She raised its glowing blue blade high and held it above the white dragon's eye as Myrddin continued his impassioned chanting.

For a brief moment, she looked up at Arturius, a sadness dimming her gray eyes, and a memory that twisted his insides and ached in his soul struck him. The death of Talara, as Viviane had shown him.

He saw Rhaegar's chest expand with air, saw the steam twisting in the air above his nostrils, so he leapt forward and clutched Talara in his front talons, shielding her from the fiery blast just in time. Though he hadn't thought of it, his body had also shielded Myrddin.

You're welcome, bard.

He set Talara carefully on the ground, then turned back to the white dragon and chomped his teeth around its neck. Talara gathered herself, readied the sword again, and waited.

Kill him, Talara! Arturius cried out telepathically, not knowing if she would hear him.

But she nodded to him, then drew the sword a little higher and plunged it into Rhaegar's eye.

The dragon's dying scream was at once deep, booming, and shrill, and the earth itself seemed to mourn the creature with a jarring tremor.

"The heart," Arturius instructed, remorse nipping at the edges of his soul as he watched Rhaegar's ethereal spirit climb from his body.

The spirit's eyes locked on him, but there was no anger in them.

We shall meet as brothers in the next world.

Arturius tried to smother the pain, a piece of his soul being ripped away as Rhaegar's spirit drifted toward the clouds, but the agony was too great. He gave a mourning bellow for the brother he'd killed, then collapsed atop his lifeless body.

When he opened his eyes, Talara didn't look so small anymore. Her face hovered over him, tears in her eyes as she stroked his hair.

"You're awake," she said through her tears, bottom lip quivering.

The memories came back a few pieces at a time. Lanslot. Gwynafar. The Saxon army.

"Rigana," he whispered, the breath leaving his lungs.

"Myrddin and Drystan are preparing her. Eilinor has come to help us take her home." Talara's tears dripped onto Arthur's cheeks, and he dragged her into his embrace. They held each other as the salt of their tears stung their faces.

He knew that defeating the white dragon was only the first step in turning the tide, but they had done it. With the help of their friends, the land, and the gods, they had won their first major victory.

Arthur wished it could be all, that he could take Talara and build a home with her in the forest on Insula Avallonis, but there were still more battles to be fought if their way of life was to be saved. They had to claim their stake in the land and come to peace with the invaders, whether through ink or blood.

Could he call the dragon again? He didn't know if he could, or if he wanted to. It was a beast that struggled to see the future or the past and rarely remembered fighting for anyone but itself. The beast was him, and he was the beast. And that dragon had terrified him.

No matter what was to come, he would face it with Talara, Myrddin, and Drystan. They had seen the best of him, and they had seen the beast, and they still held him as their leader. But their next battle would have to wait until they buried their dead and mourned the passing of those they'd lost.

They burned the bodies of Lanslot and the native dead, then gently prepared Rigana's body for travel. Drystan found some riderless horses roaming the battlefield, and they set out for Caer Cadwyr together.

Myrddin's once happy ditties about drunken brawls and cuckolded husbands gave way to songs of blood-soaked glory and noble sacrifice as they rode west across the battle-ravaged land. Here and there, in the deepest shadows and in the high branches of trees, Arthur spotted the ravens. Watching him, studying what was left of his closest companions, he had no doubt those black-feathered messengers of the Morrigan kept a close eye on him for their master.

Glossary

Aelwen – A skilled archer in Arthur's warband.

Anieras – A powerful druid and one of the last of an ancient order, preserving the old ways in a world increasingly dominated by war and foreign influences.

Aquila Catuvellaunus – King of Calleva Atrebatum, a key ally of Arthur.

Arthur – The familiar and personal name by which Arthur is addressed by his closest companions and followers. In legend and historical speculation, Arthur is depicted as a post-Roman war leader resisting Saxon invasions.

Arturius – The Latinized form of Arthur's name, reflective of the Romano-British world he inhabited. A cross inscribed with "rex Arturius" (amid a longer, Latin inscription) was reportedly discovered by monks at Glastonbury in the 12th century with the remains of a man and a woman. The authenticity of the findings at Glastonbury are disputed. Regardless, this discovery was later tied to the legend of Arthur's final resting place.

Brosca (River Brosca) – The pre-Saxon name of the River Brue, which runs through Somerset and is linked to Arthur's journey.

Caer Cadwyr – A fortified site inspired by Cadbury Castle, a location often linked to Arthurian legend and historically thought to be an ancient Roman fortification. Located near the village of South

Cadbury in Somerset, England, this site has a long history stretching back to Roman times and beyond. It is considered a possible location for the mythic Camelot, tying this ancient stronghold to legendary battles.

Calleva Atrebatum – A major Roman-British town, once the center of the Atrebates tribe. Located in modern Silchester, Hampshire, it remained an important settlement after the Roman withdrawal, with archaeological evidence indicating continued habitation and fortifications. In *Arturius*, it is ruled by Aquila Catuvellaunus as a bastion of native resistance.

Cymru (KUM-ree) – The native Welsh name for Wales, referring to the lands of the Britons resisting Saxon invasion. The people of Cymru are called Cymry(KUM-ree).

Cynhyrfedd (KUN-hur-veth) – A massive black wolf with glowing red eyes, considered an omen or a guide.

Din Gwiddon – The village of witches led by Eilinor, located near Lake Llyn Llydaw in the mountains of Wales. This secluded, prehistoric-styled settlement serves as a sanctuary for those who practice the old ways, preserving ancient magical traditions and wisdom.

Drystan – One of Arthur's closest friends and warriors.

Dux Bellorum – A Latin title meaning "Leader of Battles." Historically, it was a recognized Roman military designation for a commander who led troops in war but did not hold the official rank of a general. In the post-Roman period, it became associated with warlords like Arthur, signifying his role as a military leader.

Eilinor – The leader of the witches at Din Gwiddon.

Excalibur – Arthur's sword, blessed or given by the Lady of the Lake.

Gwayw (GWY-you) – A spear used in Celtic and Brythonic warfare, originating from a Brythonic root meaning 'spear' or 'javelin.'

Gwynafar – Arthur's third wife, whose marriage solidifies a critical alliance.

Kernow (KER-now) – The Brythonic name for Cornwall. The people of Kernow are called Kernowek (KER-now-ek).

King Stone – A solitary standing stone traditionally associated with kingship and burial rites. Part of the Rollright Stones complex, it is believed to have served as a marker of power and transition between the earthly and spiritual realms have served.

King's Men – A stone circle within the Rollright Stones, believed to be a Bronze Age ceremonial site. Tales from folklore tell of a group of warriors turned to stone, linking them to legends of lost armies and supernatural events.

Lanslot – Arthur's childhood friend and a formidable warrior.

Morrigan – An ancient Celtic goddess of death, battle, fate, and sovereignty, and often associated with war and prophecy. She can appear as an omen before great conflicts. Reputedly, she would appear at bodies of water, washing the armor of warriors who were soon to die in battle

Myrddin – A druid and seer who serves as a counselor to Arthur. Inspired by Myrddin Wyllt, who is believed to have later been adapted by Geoffrey of Monmouth as Merlin.

Rigana – A skilled warrior and the first of Arthur's wives.

Saxons – An early Germanic people originating from what is now northern Germany. By the 5th century CE, they invaded/migrated to Britain alongside the Angles and Jutes, playing a major role in shaping post-Roman Britain.

Spatha – A long, straight-bladed sword of Roman origin, commonly used by cavalry.

Talara – Arthur's second wife, skilled with a bow.

Tegid – The ancient king whose spirit is tied to the King Stone.

Tintagel – A prominent coastal fortress in Cornwall, often associated with Arthurian legend. The site features extensive remains of post-Roman structures, making it a likely seat of power for native rulers and a busy hub for maritime trade.

Viviane (Lady of the Lake) – A mystical figure who grants Arthur wisdom and guidance.

Whispering Warriors – The third and final formation within the Rollright Stones, a dolmen better known as the Whispering Knights. The name was altered in this story to reflect the pre-knightly era of Arthur's time. These stones are often associated with mystical energies and prophecy, believed to carry echoes of ancient rituals and divine communications.

Ynys Witrin (IN-is WIT-rin) (Insula Avallonis) – A sacred island and key location in Arthur's legend, known later (and more commonly) as Avalon.

Twisted Tales of Familiar Faces

If you enjoyed this dark retelling of the *King Aruthur* legend, don't miss out on the rest of this horrifying collection!

Humbug (Scrooge) - Andre Gonzalez

Sweethaven (Popeye) - RJ Clark

Timber Beast (Paul Bunyan) - A.K. Hughey

Alice (Alice in Wonderland) - Audrey Brice

Wish (Aladdin) - Courtney Konstantin

Quixote (Don Quixote) - Stephen Wertzbaugher

Arturius (King Arthur) - A.K. Hughey

Steamboat (Steamboat Willie) - Courtney Konstantin

Strangled (Rapunzel) - Stephen Wertzbaugher

Dethroning Oz (Wizard of Oz) - Audrey Brice

Scorned (Hercules) - Z.S. Diamanti

Check out the entire collection at www.m4lpublishing.com

Join our newsletter to stay up to date with all upcoming releases at www.m4lpublishing.com

Author's Note

First and foremost, my deepest gratitude goes to the storytellers of the past—those whose voices have been lost through the millennia, yet whose lives and stories continue to echo through the ages. Their hardships, tragedies, and victories inspire me daily.

To those who encouraged me—especially Julie, Randy, Nan, and Niki—when the shadows of doubt crept in, thank you for your unwavering support. Your words and presence light my path through the dark moments.

To my husband for sharing a love of all things ancient and classical history with me.

To my editor, Nan, whose eye for detail and shared love of history helped shape my winding thoughts, you have my everlasting appreciation. Your feedback was invaluable, and you see what so many others might easily miss.

To my family, who endured my time lost in the world of this book, thank you for your patience, love, and understanding—and for celebrating with me when I finished.

And finally, to two of my favorite professors, Dr. Leslie Kelly and Dr. Michael Ng, whose instruction, guidance, and encouragement nurtured my love of history and deepened my understanding of the past.

Enjoy this book?

We hope you enjoyed this release from M4L Publishing.

Reviews are the most helpful tools in getting new readers for any books. We don't have the financial backing of a New York publishing house and can't afford to blast our books on billboards or bus stops.

(Not yet!)

That said, your honest review can go a long way in helping us reach new readers. If you've enjoyed this book, we'd be forever grateful if you could spend a couple minutes leaving it a review (it can be as short as you like) on the site you purchased this book from.

Thank you so much!

About the author

A.K. Hughey invokes her B.A. in English and M.A. in Ancient and Classical History to craft chilling horror tales steeped in culture and dripping with lore. Specializing in paranormal and historical horror, along with vigilante thrillers, she weaves stories that captivate and terrify. Residing in the cryptid-filled heart of Appalachia, A.K. stalks the eerie landscape for inspiration and shares her home with her family and her feline overlords.

www.ingramcontent.com/pod-product-compliance
Lightning Source LLC
Chambersburg PA
CBHW030858200726

48289CB00003B/808